In Plain Sight

In Plain Sight

Carol Otis Hurst

Houghton Mifflin Company Boston 2002

Walter Lorraine Books

For Rebecca and Jill
— gold I didn't have to search for

Walter Lorraine (wr) Books

www.houghtonmifflinbooks.com

Library of Congress Cataloging-in-Publication Data

Hurst, Carol Otis.
  In plain sight / Carol Otis Hurst.
      p. cm.
Summary: Eleven-year-old Sarah copes with emotional and
economic hardships when her beloved but impulsive father leaves
the family and their Massachusetts farm to prospect for gold in
California.
  ISBN 0-618-19699-4
  [1. Farm life—Massachusetts—Fiction. 2. Family
life—Massachusetts—Fiction. 3. Fathers—Fiction. 4.
Massachusetts—Fiction.] I. Title.
  PZ7.H95678 In 2002
  [Fic]—dc21

                                    2001004427

Printed in the U.S.A.
QUM 10 9 8 7 6 5 4 3 2 1

CONTENTS

1

Talking of Gold

With a sigh of relief, Sarah stood. The edge of the hard wooden pew had been digging into the backs of her legs for the past two hours. It felt so good to stretch her legs at last. She turned in time to catch a warning glance from her mother. Oh, sugar! Her mother had heard her sigh. All those hours of sitting still were gone to waste. All her mother would remember was that sigh. Nothing for it now but to pretend everything was fine. Her mother's standards of behavior at church — and everywhere else, for that matter — were hard to live up to.

Rachel and Robbie had each caught not only the dreaded glance of disapproval that Sarah had just earned but occasional slaps on their legs as the endless service had gone on. Being so much younger than she at five and seven years old, they at least had been allowed to practice their letters on the back of the church calendar. Sarah, now eleven, was held to a higher standard. She leaned forward now to watch her father stand. With a wink at Sarah, he not only sighed but also stretched his arms high and wide. Then he rubbed his backside.

"Miles!" her mother whispered, nudging him with her elbow.

"Sorry, Delina," he murmured, "but my sit-down's sore."

Sarah grinned, hearing her mother sigh as she followed him into the aisle. There was no controlling Miles Corbin. He took Rachel and Robbie by the hand as the family took its place behind the Carters and proceeded slowly from the church.

"Over here, Miles!" Mr. Allyn was waving from a group of men standing in the churchyard. Rachel and Robbie ran off to join children in a game of tag already starting up in the long grass alongside the church. Sarah was torn between the game and the conversation of the men. There was already a shout of laughter from something her father had said. She took a step in that direction.

"Sarah," said her mother quietly, putting a hand on Sarah's arm.

The choice was made for her. Sarah hid her disappointment and walked beside her mother as she approached the group of women who seemed to have nothing more interesting to talk about than the lack of rain and the gardens. It had been a long, dry summer, but did they have to go on and on about it?

Sarah glanced over at the men. Their conversation was bound to be about things more exciting than this — probably California. That's all everyone — except these boring ladies — talked about these days. There was gold in California — lots of it. Many men had already left Westfield and other towns in western Massachusetts to join the rush for gold. Some were to make the long trek across the plains; others were going by ship around Cape Horn. Sarah thought that either way would be a thrilling adventure.

"Is Miles really going to go to California?" asked Mrs. Standish.

Sarah's head snapped up. Going? Her father? No! Surely not!

"Says he is," her mother said.

"When?" asked Mrs. Carter. Sarah held her breath.

"When and if he gets enough money, I suppose."

Sarah slowly exhaled. Money in their family was never plentiful. She didn't think they could really be called poor because of the farm. On it they raised enough food for the family to get by most years, but actual cash was as scarce as hen's teeth. Getting together enough cash to make the journey to California would surely take her father a long time, probably forever.

"But Delina," Mrs. Carter said, "what will you and the children do if he goes?"

"We'll manage. We always have. Come along, Sarah. Time to get dinner started." Her mother turned and walked toward her husband.

"Mother —" Sarah started the question but her mother ignored her. Sarah hurried to catch up.

There was another shout of laughter as they approached the men, and Mr. Lane slapped her father on the back. "Good one, Miles," he said. The laughter stopped as Sarah and her mother approached.

"Morning, ladies," Mr. Cook said, tipping his hat.

Her mother nodded briefly. "Gentlemen. Miles," she said, "time to go."

"Right you are, Delina," her father said cheerfully. He turned back to the men. "Stop by this evening," he said. "We'll talk more then."

The others waved and nodded, tipped their hats to her mother, and wandered slowly off toward their own families.

Her father put his hand on his wife's elbow, helping her step up into the wagon. He turned to Sarah, but she already had her foot on the top rim of the wheel and was clambering into the back.

"Sarah!" said her mother. "Use the step and your father's arm. You're eleven years old. Act like a lady, for once in your life."

"Yes, Mother," Sarah said softly. She certainly didn't need to be helped up into the wagon, for goodness' sake. It seemed like everything she did this morning just gave her mother another chance to disapprove. Acting like a lady wasn't much fun. She remembered when she thought it was, dressing up in her mother's shoes and discarded clothes when she was Rachel's age. Growing up had seemed like a lot of fun back then. Now that she was nearly grown up, Sarah was not so sure. She not only had more chores to do than Robbie and Rachel did, she seemed to be running short on the fun. She glanced at her mother as she settled onto her bench and wondered if her mother ever had fun. She worked hard — Sarah knew and appreciated that — but she never laughed, seldom even smiled. Her father seemed to enjoy himself, though.

Her father's piercing whistle stopped any further thoughts. In the field Robbie and Rachel's heads snapped up and they ran toward the wagon.

"Miles!" her mother said sharply. "We're at church, for pity's sake."

"Correction, Delina," he said. "We were at church. Now, thank the good Lord, we are out of it."

Rachel and Robbie scrambled into the wagon, their father clicked his tongue and slapped the reins gently on Dorcas's back, and the big horse began his slow trot toward home.

Sarah looked forward to Sunday afternoons. School and chores took up most weekdays. Saturday their mother kept everybody hopping and chores chewed up that day, but Sunday afternoon, once the clean-up from the big noonday dinner was done, was free time.

"Hide-and-seek!" Robbie shouted as soon as the last dish was dried and put away. He ran out the door. "Not it!"

"Not it!" Rachel echoed, running after him. Sarah laughed and went to the big elm tree in the front yard. Putting her face into her crooked arm as she leaned against the tree, she began to count as they ran off.

". . . ninety-eight, ninety-nine, one hundred!" she called at last. "Here I come, ready or not. Anyone around my goal is it!"

She turned to see her mother step onto the porch and sit in the rocker, taking up her darning. Her father sat on the step beside her, watching them.

Sarah saw Rachel peering out from behind the milk room but pretended she had not. She ran off to find Robbie first. In a few minutes she spotted him crouched on the big limb of the maple. "I see you, Robbie!" she called. She ran back to the elm, touching it as she yelled, "Robbie's goal, one, two, three!"

Now she was off to find Rachel as Robbie clambered down. Sarah ran around the milk room but Rachel wasn't there. Cautiously she opened the door. It was cool inside, and the smell of fresh milk was strong. The milk cans stood full in the ice bin, ready for tomorrow's pickup. Sarah turned to go, and then spotted Rachel curled up in a corner of the bin.

"Oh, Rachel," she said. "Come out of there before you . . ."

She reached out, but not in time to grasp the large eight-gallon container as it tipped, spilling most of its contents into the ice bin. Rachel froze, her hands on the edge of the bin, her legs dangling behind her.

"Oops!" she said. Instantly her eyes filled with tears. "I didn't mean to."

"No, of course you didn't," Sarah said, lifting her down and putting her arm around her.

"Let's not tell Mama," Rachel said, looking at Sarah hopefully.

"We have to," Sarah said. "But let's clean it up first." Sarah picked up the mop and climbed into the ice bin.

"But she'll be mad," Rachel's chin quivered again.

"I know." Sarah opened the drain to let the milk and water flow out onto the ground. "The barn cats will get a feast," she said.

By the time Sarah had finished cleaning up and walked onto the porch, neither Rachel nor Robbie was anywhere in sight.

"Game all over?" asked her father.

"Well, there was a little accident," Sarah said,

looking at her mother.

"What's happened now?" she asked.

"A milk can got knocked over."

"My land!" her mother said. "Can't I have a moment's peace?" She stood and made a move toward the milk room.

"Now, Delina," said her father. "They were just playing. I'll bet Sarah has it all cleaned up. Right, Sarie?"

Sarah smiled gratefully at her father. "Yup," she said.

"That's my girl," he said.

"And what about the lost milk?" her mother asked.

He grinned. "No use crying over it," he said, coming to his feet as his wife rolled her eyes. "Come on, Sarah. I challenge you to a game of checkers."

2

Gathering Funds

"Here's my fifty."

Sarah softly closed her bedroom door and crept out to the top step to listen to the men's conversation below. Robbie and Rachel were sound asleep.

"You'll get it back, Jeff, with more to go with it." Her father's voice was firm.

"Oh, you've got it right, Miles," Mr. Axtel said, as Sarah gathered her nightgown around her legs and bare feet to keep warm. It was cold, even for late October. "Gold's the only thing that'll take us out of the mess we're in. Taxes are high and there's no work to speak of."

"Plenty of gold in California." Mr. Gillett's voice was squeaky with excitement. "Why, it's just lying on the street waiting for folks to pick it up! You'll find plenty, Miles. No trouble at all."

"Says in the paper even President Polk wants people to come get the gold." Sarah couldn't make out whose voice that was. "You know California is already a territory."

"You betcha!" Her father spoke again. There was no confusing his booming voice. "It'll be a state 'fore long."

Mr. Sanford spoke up next. "I heard tell of a man

who found so much gold he couldn't carry it all to town in a wheelbarrow. Pieces kept falling out as he ran to the assayer's office to stake his claim. Just lying on the ground it was, ready for the taking!"

"Shucks!" said another voice. "You won't even have to find it yourself, Miles. We can all get rich on somebody else's leavings!"

"You got enough to book passage yet, Miles?" It was Mr. Axtel's question. Sarah held her breath.

"Just about," her father said.

Sarah put her hand over her mouth to keep from yelling out a protest. He couldn't have enough money. Where had it come from?

As if he had heard her thoughts, her father went on.

"I've got our savings, of course, and a couple of loans came through. Those, together with the money you've brought tonight, ought to be enough."

"Great!" Mr. Allyn said. "We'll make our money without leaving Westfield. I can't leave the store. Staking you is the perfect solution, Miles."

Then Sarah heard her mother's voice, rising above the excited voices of the men. "If it is so easy to find gold in California, why is it that none of you can name one single person who has come back here with so much as a nugget?"

It was just like her mother to throw cold water on

their plans, but for once Sarah hoped it would work.

"They're still out there," Mr. Gillett squeaked, "getting more!"

"Delina," her father exclaimed, "we're going to be rich! Everybody's going to be rich!"

"Bah! Pipe dreams!" said her mother. "It's a fool's errand, Miles, and you're the fool to go on it!"

Sarah stepped quickly into her own room as she heard her mother's angry footsteps start up the stairs.

Sarah lay in her bed, trying to steady her breathing and keep her eyelids from fluttering as her mother stopped in the doorway. Her eyes flew open again as she heard the door to her parents' room open and close.

Her father must have promised those men a share of his find in return for their money. It hurt her chest to even think about it, but her father was going to California.

The next morning Sarah dampened a towel and patted her eyes. Her nose was bright red, and her eyes swollen nearly shut. She knew she looked terrible. She'd cried most of the night.

Her father looked up as Sarah came down into the kitchen. She turned away quickly but not soon enough.

"You heard, Sarah?"

She turned to him. She couldn't speak but nodded

as she searched his face for some sign that he had changed his mind. His look and that of her mother as she turned from the stove to place more griddlecakes on the table told Sarah that the decision was final. He was leaving — leaving the farm, leaving Westfield, leaving them all behind.

Her mother motioned Sarah to her seat and sat down at the table herself. Without a word, she picked up her fork and began to eat.

"It's all decided, Sarie," her father said cheerfully. He leaned over to put his arm around her. "I'll leave in two weeks." He smiled sadly at Sarah's intake of breath. "I won't be gone long," he said. "You'll barely have time to miss me."

Sarah could hear Robbie and Rachel's footsteps overhead. They'd be down in a minute. She took her napkin from its ring and placed it in her lap, head down, too full of tears to speak.

Sarah spent as much of each of the next aching days as possible in her father's presence. Each night Sarah had to be told several times that it was time for bed, and she went up only after lingering goodnights, reassurances, and hugs. She rose each morning as soon as she heard his tread in the kitchen, anxious not to miss a precious minute of his company.

Lying awake in her room night after night, Sarah

strained to hear her mother and father talking in the kitchen. Usually they talked too quietly for her to make out the words.

Sarah gave up reading the newspaper. It was filled with more talk about the gold rush. Before this it had been exciting to read about it. There were ads for passage and supplies all over the *Springfield Union*. And there were articles about those who had made or were making the trip. No matter which route people took, according to the paper, just getting to California was very dangerous and took many months. What had been exciting reading now had become torture. She couldn't bear to read about the dangers her very own father would soon face.

Sarah knew that the prospect of a hazardous trip wasn't enough to stop her father or any of the others who wanted gold. Times were hard here in western Massachusetts. The canal, which had promised so much to the area, was closed; the corporation dissolved. Many investors had lost all their money. One of those investors was Sarah's father. Sarah knew that was part of her father's determination to join the crowd of forty-niners heading to California, but she also knew that her father was as anxious for the adventure as he was for the gold.

"Father," Sarah said one evening as she snuggled beside him on the settee (she'd have climbed into his lap if she didn't think eleven was a bit old for that), "why can't we all go? The Meyers left last spring — Mrs. Meyer and the baby and Helmut — they all went. Helmut said they'd buy their oxen and wagon in Missouri and join up with a wagon train there. Why can't we do that? Please, Father, please?"

Her father kissed the top of her head. "Your mother's not up to it, Sarah."

"You mean she won't go," said Sarah, pulling away angrily and turning to face her father.

"All right," he agreed, nodding sadly. "She won't go."

"Then take me, Father." She flung herself back into his arms. "I can help with the oxen. I'm strong, Father, strong enough to walk to California."

He shook his head as he stroked her hair. "Your mother would never allow it."

"She spoils everything!"

He turned her face to look at his. "I agree with her, Sarah. It's a long, dangerous journey no matter which route you take, and California's not a place for decent women and children. Anyway, I'm not going by wagon train. I'm taking the Panama route. And a ship is no place for a pretty young thing like you, Sarah, no matter how strong you are. It'll be full of men. Some of them will be pretty tough sorts."

"The Meyers —"

"The Meyers are immigrants," he said. "Westfield isn't home for them. They came here to work on the canal and it's closed. Karl Meyer has neither job nor property here. That's why they're all going west. You've got a home here on a farm that's been in my family for generations. It's not fancy," he said, "but it's done all right."

"Then go a different way," said Sarah. "Don't go by boat."

"It's the quickest way to the Pacific." Taking her hand, he led her to the desk. Rachel and Robbie left their game of jacks to squeeze in front of them as their father carefully unfolded a map and traced the route with his finger. "I'll board ship in Boston. That's here. We'll go down the Atlantic coast, probably never even get out of land sight, to Panama. Along here and here. Think of all the sights I'll see! There'll be monkeys and parrots. It'll be a regular traveling circus, but I'll be the traveler!"

"Where are the monkeys?" Rachel asked, pushing his hand out of the way. "I don't see any monkeys."

"Of course you can't see them!" Robbie said with disgust. "It's a map."

Rachel's lower lip quivered, and her father put his left arm around her as he pointed to a wiggly black line on a narrow neck of land. "No monkeys here, Rache, but there's a river. See that little black line?"

"Doesn't look like a river," Rachel said.

Robbie sighed and rolled his eyes. With a wink at his son, his father went on. "Then, here at Panama, we'll go seventy-five miles up the Chagres River, take a mule train the other twenty-five miles, and there I'll be on the West Coast!" He jabbed at the map with his finger. "Think of it, children, the Pacific Ocean, then California and all that gold."

Robbie's and even Rachel's eyes shone with excitement, but Sarah's were full of tears.

Miles Corbin put his arms around three children. "Besides," he said. "I want to see the elephant."

"The elephant? You don't have to go to California to see an elephant," Sarah said, blinking away the tears. "Wait till the circus comes through Westfield."

Her father grinned. "There's a story going 'round about the farmer who heard that an elephant was coming to town with the circus. Now, he had never seen an elephant, and so he loaded his wagon with produce, hitched up the horse, and headed to town to sell his goods and to see the elephant.

"Just before he got to town, what should he see right on the road but the elephant being led by its keeper. The farmer was delighted. Unfortunately, his horse had never seen an elephant, either. The horse shied, upsetting the cart with the farmer in it, and ran off. Even so, as he picked himself up and surveyed his

ruined produce, the farmer declared, 'It was worth it!
I have seen the elephant.'"

"Oh, I like that story," said Robbie.

"What happened to the elephant?" Rachel asked.

Her father grinned. "I expect he had a good story
to tell the other elephants."

"That's a nice story," Sarah said, "but what has it
to do with going to California?"

"Sarie, in California I'll see the elephant and cover
him with gold!"

"What will we do with all that gold?" Rachel
wondered.

"I could get a new fishing pole," Robbie said.

"You sure could," said their father. He rubbed the
top of Robbie's head.

"And dolls! I get a doll?" Rachel said.

"With all that gold," their father said, laughing,
"the sky's the limit. We'll have gold, gold, gold." He
snatched up Rachel and held her high over his head.
She squealed with delight.

"Gold, gold, gold, gold!" Robbie began to chant
as their father put Rachel back down. She began to
make drumming noises and led a march around the
room. Their father joined them, pulling Robbie into
line and grinning broadly as he stamped out the
rhythm. "Come on!" he cried. "Join the gold parade."

Sarah stood watching them without a smile.

3

Leaving

They followed the railroad tracks that bordered their land, crossed the river, and cut through the fields to the depot. Sarah clung to her father's hand, making no attempt to stop the tears that ran down her cheeks and nose and fell to the ground. With a strange fascination she watched the drops disappear in the dirt as her footsteps erased their traces.

Only Rachel seemed to share Sarah's despair. She had her father's other hand and had been sobbing loudly since she got up that morning.

Robbie, on the other hand, was overjoyed to be this close to the trains he loved. He hopped along, balancing on the rail with one foot in the air until their mother made him stop. Delina Corbin walked with her head down, her lips tight, arms folded across her waist. Whatever her thoughts were on that cold November day, she kept them to herself. Rags trotted alongside Robbie, glad to be on an outing with his family. He disappeared now and again in search of rabbits but quickly rejoined the group, his tail wagging.

Sarah glanced at her father. There was no sadness there. He had a spring in his step and was whistling. Sarah could make out the tune to "Oh! Susanna."

Waiting for the train was an awful time. They stomped their feet with the cold as they stepped into the station, hoping for warmth, but it was almost as cold inside as out. They held their hands out to the little stove that radiated heat only for a foot or so.

No one made an attempt at conversation. Sarah was glad of that, for her throat was so choked with tears that she couldn't have spoken had she tried. Rachel sobbed, and even Robbie cried when the conductor's "All aboard!" put an end to the agony. Miles Corbin put his arms around his children and held them tightly. He held each child's face as he kissed it, kissed his wife on the cheek, and then, grinning broadly, he boarded the train. The children watched him through the windows as he took a seat. He gave one quick wave and almost immediately the whistle blew. There was a puff of steam and, just that quickly, he was gone.

His children watched until the train was out of sight, holding on to one another as they cried. When Sarah lifted her head at last, she saw that their mother was already striding toward home. Rags waited patiently by the door of the station.

The days that followed were full of tears. Even Rags went about with his head and tail down. Each evening the dog sniffed at her father's chair before settling down by the fire. For Sarah it seemed that her tears were always ready to fall. She would sob for a time, then gather herself together, taking up her chores. Then some sight, sound, or smell would remind her of her father and the tears would come full force again.

She told herself over and over that it wasn't forever. He *was* coming back, after all. That's what everyone who tried to comfort her said, but nothing could change the awful truth. He wasn't here. And she wanted him back, needed him now. She felt friendless and alone without him. She moved about the house as if she were walking through syrup.

How did the others do it, she wondered? Rachel and Robbie seemed sad at times, of course, but they played or did their chores as usual. She even heard them laughing out loud sometimes. As far as Sarah knew, her mother had not shed a tear after or before her husband left. Delina Corbin went about her work, same as always, seeming to ignore the empty chair at the table, the awful silence of the long evenings.

Sarah stared at her mother sometimes, wondering how she managed it. Once in a while her mother turned and caught her at it. "What? What is it, Sarah? Is my face dirty?"

"No."

"Then what is it?"

"Nothing," Sarah would say, looking away.

Each night just before bed, Robbie and Rachel asked for reassurance from Sarah that their father was coming back. When would that be and how long must they wait, they wanted to know. But, during the day, they seemed to forget about him. To Sarah, the laughter of Robbie and Rachel at play was as incomprehensible as her mother's silence. As for herself, Sarah didn't think she'd ever laugh again.

As the days went by, images of her father seemed to grow larger than life. How often neighbors and friends had come to talk with him. In good weather, the men had played horseshoes, laughing and joking all the while. The women had watched and cheered them on or sat and sewed together, engaged in quiet talk. Those were good times for them all. They'd had few visitors since her father had left.

How he had loved company, Sarah remembered — the bigger the group, the better. His laughter shouted. His voice boomed. His stories had held everyone spellbound. He loved to sing, and, when he began, others simply had to join in, even if they didn't know all the verses. She'd even heard her mother join in once and was surprised that her voice was lovely, a high, clear soprano.

But all that had stopped — the music, the laughter, and the stories. Miles Corbin was gone.

4

The Plan

Their father might be gone, but the work remained. The routines of life went right on. After and before school and on weekends, there were chores. The cows needed to be milked twice a day. Sarah and her mother did that. Rachel gathered the eggs and fed the chickens. Robbie fed and brushed Dorcas, and mucked out the barn. Their mother cooked, cleaned, and ran the house. They all worked at turning the wool to yarn. That work tided the household through the winter, but soon the fields would have to be plowed and planted. Sarah wasn't strong enough to handle the plow. She doubted that her mother could do it either. What if their father didn't come back in time to do the spring planting? What would they do then?

The children waited anxiously for the mail each day, looking for letters that did not come.

"Sarah," Robbie said one night, "I think the reason we haven't heard from Father is that he got to California right away and found the gold and now he's on his way back. That's why he hasn't written. He's too busy."

"Maybe." Sarah put her arm around him. "Sometimes the mail has trouble getting through," she said. "I don't imagine there are many post offices in California."

"Do you think he's seen the elephant?"

Sarah smiled, remembering the story. "Maybe."

"Why don't we write a letter to him?" asked Rachel. "I'll bet he's lonesome for us. He probably thinks about us at night when he goes to bed and he probably has trouble going to sleep because he's thinking too hard about us."

Robbie whirled around. "We can't write to him, stupid! We don't know where he is!" Robbie turned and ran up to his room.

Sarah knelt in front of Rachel and brushed away her sister's tears.

"I'm not stupid." Rachel looked after Robbie with her hands on her hips.

"No, Rachel, you're not stupid. Robbie shouldn't have said that. He didn't mean it. He's just worried about Father. We all are."

"I really miss him, Sarah."

"I know, Rachel, I know."

"Father will be back soon, won't he?"

"Soon," Sarah answered. She wished she were sure of that.

Sarah couldn't talk about her own fears to anyone. She didn't want to upset Robbie and Rachel, and she was afraid to show her mother any such weakness. It seemed disloyal, somehow, not to have faith in her father. Surely he'd be home by planting time.

The weather grew warmer and then colder again in early March as spring tried and failed to come. Mud was everywhere. The food in the cellar would thaw and then refreeze. They had to eat most of the pork before it spoiled. That was food her mother had planned to keep until later in the spring and early summer, the hard time between planting and first crop.

Sarah watched her mother as the weeks went by. Mrs. Corbin had always seemed remote, slow to laugh and quick to scold. Now she seemed even more distant. Things had never been easy between them. Sarah watched mothers at church or on the street comforting their children. Her mother must have done that when she was little but she wasn't at all sure. It seemed as if she had always known that her mother was a woman to be approached with caution even in the best of times, her reaction usually stern.

There was little time for talk or play between chores and school, but, if the children hurried home and whisked through chores, they could have a few minutes to play in the barn or to ride Dorcas through the fields. Things seemed almost all right then. The hard times were the evenings, which had once seemed filled with laughter. Now there was mostly silence.

Sarah read most evenings, sometimes aloud to the younger children as they played endless turns of cat's cradle and other string games. Their mother pored over the account books or wove on the loom.

Coming in from milking one evening in late March, Sarah heard the spring peepers in the pond. She stopped and listened, cheered by this sign of spring and, when she entered the house, she was singing made-up words about the peepers to a tune she'd heard somewhere. Her mother was sitting at the kitchen table, the account books open before her.

"Will you stop that incessant noise!" she said without looking up.

Sarah's good mood vanished immediately. She stood stock-still in the center of the room.

Her mother took a deep breath and motioned to the chair at the table. "Sarah," her mother said, "sit down. I've something to tell you."

"Is it Father?" There was a flicker of hope. No one knew if he had even reached the gold fields. News had trickled back about two other gold-seekers from Westfield, Jess and Daniel Otis. Their families had quickly spread the news that they had arrived in California and were panning for gold on the American River. Maybe now there was word of her father.

"No, not your father." Mrs. Corbin took a deep breath and then went on. "Sarah, we're coming very close to losing this place."

"Losing?" For a moment Sarah's mind refused to deal with it. "The farm? What do you mean 'losing'?"

Her mother looked straight at her. "I can no longer pay our creditors."

"Creditors? What creditors? Are we in debt? How did we get in debt?"

"Your father took some loans."

"I know that. The neighbors gave him money for the trip. He'll pay them back even more as soon as he finds the gold. Don't they know that?"

"That's as may be," her mother said. "There are bank creditors, too, Sarah. Your father . . ." She stopped for a moment and then continued. "A search for gold was not the first scheme your father has come up with." Delina drew a breath and then looked directly into Sarah's eyes. "We are deeply in debt. We need money, so I'm going to work at the whip factory."

Sarah's eyes widened. Westfield Whip was the biggest building in town. All kinds of whips were made there and shipped around the world. The factory, standing alongside the river, with its high small windows, seemed to Sarah a dreadful thing, more of a prison than a place to work. She had seen women, their hair piled high on their heads, wearing white shirtwaists and dark skirts, lined up outside the factory in the early morning, standing apart from the men, who entered by a different door. She'd pitied them all, hearing the roar of the machinery inside. She couldn't imagine anyone choosing to work in such a place, let alone her mother.

"You can't go to work at the whip factory!" she said.

Her mother smiled grimly. "I can and I will," she said. "I can make six dollars a week there, Sarah. We can't get by any longer on what we have here. Your father took what little we had laid by."

"Well, of course he took the money. He needs it, doesn't he?" Sarah rose quickly to her father's defense.

Delina's voice remained calm. "Yes, Sarah, he needs it. But we need money too — money to hire someone to plant and plow and harvest flax."

"Flax! We've never raised flax."

"No, we have not, but that's the biggest money crop for this land."

"All right then, we'll raise flax." Sarah knew nothing about raising flax, but how hard could it be?

Her mother shook her head. "Sarah, raising flax is heavy work. You and I can't do it. We're just not strong enough. If I make some money, we can get Hiram Beech. He's looking for work, I hear. With him to work the farm, we can raise flax, sell some to pay down the loans, and still have some for our own use."

"Won't Grandfather —?"

Mrs. Corbin's head came up quickly. She looked directly at Sarah. "We will handle this, Sarah." She turned back to the books. "But it means big changes here. I will leave for the factory by six-thirty every morning and not be home until evening." She looked again at Sarah. "That means the brunt of the work here will fall upon you."

"Robbie and Rachel —"

"Can stay with the Strongs." Her mother was ready for her and finished the sentence. "I will leave them off each morning and pick them up on the way home."

"The Strongs! They can't stay with them. Mr. Strong's all right, but Mrs. Strong doesn't even like children."

"You don't know that, Sarah."

"I do know that! She always turns up her nose when she sees us . . . as if we smell bad."

"Sarah, you must learn not to judge people so harshly." Her mother shook her head.

Sarah reached out, nearly touching her mother's

hand. "I tell you, Mother, she doesn't like us. Mrs. Strong always shushes us, even when we whisper. Why, once she grabbed Rachel by the ear and marched her back home, with Rachel crying so hard she couldn't talk."

"What had Rachel done?" her mother asked, looking up again.

"Stepped into their garden to get her ball. She didn't even step on any plants." Just thinking about it made Sarah angry.

"Where was I?" her mother said.

"I don't know. At Grandfather's maybe," Sarah said. "Father met Mrs. Strong at the gate and said he'd take care of it."

"What did he do?"

Sarah grinned. "He hugged Rachel and then played ball with her."

Her mother nodded. "Of course," she said. "He's good at that."

"What do you mean?" Sarah's voice rose. She hated it when her mother criticized her father.

"Hold your tongue, young lady," her mother said. "Remember to whom you speak."

"I don't care! You never say nice things about him. I'll bet you're glad he's gone!"

The slap came hard and so quickly that Sarah wasn't ready for it. She turned and ran up the stairs to her bed, sobbing less with pain than with humiliation.

After a while, Sarah dried her tears and lay back on her bed. With no one to comfort her, crying seemed pointless. She thought about the changes her mother's decision to go to work would bring. There was no use arguing with her mother. She must have been planning this for some time. Obviously she'd been to the factory and she had worked something out with the Strongs. First her father was gone, now her mother would be gone most of the time. Sarah couldn't have Robbie and Rachel go off, too.

When she came back into the kitchen, her mother was seated at the table going over the ledger.

"Mother," Sarah said. "I'm sorry."

Delina nodded without looking up.

Sarah sat down in the chair opposite her. "By the end of next week school will be out. It won't start again until after planting season. Rachel and Robbie can stay here. They can help me until school starts. Please don't make them go to the Strongs'. We'll get on just fine."

Her mother looked up with a skeptical half smile. "You think it's easy, do you?"

"No, Mother, I know it's hard work and I probably can't do it as well as you, but we can get by."

"I will not have this place go to ruin and I will not

have my children running wild."

"They won't run wild, Mother. I can do it."

Mrs. Corbin gazed at her daughter for a moment, then nodded.

"All right. I can help some in the evenings, but not much," she said. "I should be able to make enough money at the factory to get Hiram over here next month to plow. We can put the cows with the Sanfords temporarily for a share of the milk and calves. If you're sure —"

"I'm sure," Sarah said. "We'll be together — except for Father. If we leave the farm, he won't know where to find us or where to send the letters."

"No," said her mother softly. "He won't know where to send the letters."

5

The Letter

Sarah had given up meeting the mail coach at the common each day. She had no time now. The work was endless. Her back and her arms ached from boiling, stirring, scrubbing, wringing, and hanging out the white wash that morning. It seemed now that her hands were always deep in harsh water. They were chapped and raw almost to her elbows.

Rachel was carefully washing the eggs and putting them in the big bowl. Sarah looked out to see Robbie trying to dig the kitchen garden. He'd been at it all morning without much success. The ground there was hard and unforgiving. As Sarah watched, Robbie jumped on the spade with both feet, and then leapt away as the handle fell, leaving only a small mark on the ground where the blade had been.

She wished she could help him but there was the color wash to do and the floor to scrub. She'd brought the pail of sand up from the sand spring and sprinkled it over the boards to get them ready for scrubbing. She'd get to the garden tomorrow.

Robbie and Rachel seldom complained about the added work, but Sarah knew that it was hard for them. They should be playing in the brook on this hot spring day, not working like slaves.

Sarah turned again to the wash. She'd lost track of time when Robbie came running in, waving an envelope. "A letter, Sarah! From Father!"

Sarah threw down her scrub brush, wiped her hands against her apron, and took the precious letter gently from Robbie's hand. He was panting too hard to speak.

"Is it really from Father?" Rachel asked, running in after him.

Robbie nodded.

"It is!" Sarah smiled broadly as she recognized her father's careful penmanship.

"Open it!" Rachel said.

Sarah nodded, putting her finger under the flap. Then she stopped, noticing the name on the envelope.

"We have to wait for Mother to come home. It's addressed to her," Sarah said regretfully. She placed the envelope in the exact center of the sideboard, where it seemed to call out to them throughout the afternoon. One after the other, each of Miles Corbin's children found time to touch, examine, and smell the envelope, picking at the seal just a tiny bit, and then, with a sigh, putting it back.

As soon as she could, Sarah left the color wash soaking in the big tub and went out to help her brother in the garden. "You chop," she said, handing him the big axe. "I'll dig."

Robbie's grin was thanks enough. They worked side by side in silence for a while.

"Do you think the letter says he's on his way home, Sarah?" Robbie wiped the sweat from his face with his shirtsleeve.

"Father's coming home?" Rachel had come out to hear just the end of Robbie's question.

Sarah shook her head. "I don't think so, Rachel, not yet."

"Maybe he is," Rachel said, putting up her chin, ready to defend her statement.

"Maybe," said Sarah, "but don't get your hopes up, Rache. Just be very glad to hear from him at last." She went back to finish the color wash.

It was nearly seven when Sarah saw her mother come in through the gate, her shoulders stooped, her head down. She stopped when she saw the clothes on the clothesline and went over for a closer inspection. Sarah hated the implied criticism. She'd done the best she could. Some stains just wouldn't come out no matter how hard she scrubbed or how long she boiled the wash. Just once she'd like to hear her mother say, "Good job, Sarah" or "Well done." She was certainly quick enough to speak when things were wrong.

Robbie ran out, followed by Rachel. "A letter, Mother! From Father!"

Delina Corbin's head snapped up. Sarah saw a smile cross her mother's face and then quickly disappear.

Dinner was ready; the stew had been slow cooking all day. Sarah had added water occasionally so it was just right, but no one wanted to eat until they read the letter.

With her children leaning over her, Mrs. Corbin opened the envelope. As she broke the seal, Sarah noticed that her mother's hands were in even worse shape than her own — bruised and cut in several places. There was a long scab along her mother's right thumb. Her mother's eyes slid over the pages while Rachel tugged at her skirt. Delina handed the letter to Sarah.

"Read it, Sarah. My eyes are tired."

Sarah needed no second invitation. She sat down at the table with Rachel on one side and Robbie close on the other. Her mother sat across the room, hands in her lap.

March 12, 1850
Panama City
My Dear Delina and Beloved Children,
I hope you are all well and missing me a little. I'm missing you all a lot. I am sorry not to have written sooner but the trip took far longer than it was

thought to take. The voyage down the Atlantic coast was slow although we stayed close to the shore to take advantage of the offshore winds. Still we were becalmed half of the time.

Folks on board ship gave me some good ideas about how to find gold once we get there so I am all ready. Some men lost their money gambling on board ship and will not be able to go on. Fortunately my luck held.

We got to the Isthmus on March 1 and then began the trip up the Chagres River. First we traveled on a steamer and then we switched to small canoes. The heat and the insects were fierce.

Drivers waited at the head with mules and guides. They were not cheap and some more men ran out of money there. My money held up and I could join the trek. I was glad of that but twenty-five miles on mule-back made my sit-down sore.

One of the fellows had a good story to tell. He said that in Devil's Creek, there was a man who owned Lightning, the meanest, most vicious mule on the whole Pacific coast. Lightning looked peaceful enough but that critter would bite and kick the nearest person whenever it was being loaded or when startled. Then that mule would set off on a run, knocking down everything and everybody in its way. It was a big joke for the men in Devil's Creek to offer

Lightning to any prospector who hadn't heard of Lightning's surprising personality. They loved to watch the city slicker pack all his belongings on the mule, yell "Giddyap!" and then see that mule go off like a house afire, biting, kicking, and stomping all over the man's gear before dashing off with the rest of it.

"Why is he going on about that foolish mule?" Delina's voice cut in.

"It's a story, Mother. You know how he likes a good story."

"So do we," Rachel said. "Go on, Sarah. What about Lightning?"

With a nervous glance at her mother, Sarah continued.

Seems that one day a man from Maine came to Devil's Creek and asked where the nearest gold was. The men snickered amongst themselves and offered him the use of Lightning. He was delighted and said he'd start out the next morning.

Bright and early, all the jokers were waiting and watching while the man packed all his grub, his tools and equipment on Lightning, who stood there patiently waiting as each thing was tied to his back and sides.

Then the man came over to shake the jokers' hands and thank them for the advice and the mule. They shook his hand but their eyes were on Lightning, who would surely bolt any minute. The man turned to Lightning and said, "Let's go, girl," and the mule walked quietly along beside him. The men all waved their hats and hollered to spook the mule. The city slicker thought they were just saying goodbye and he waved back. Lightning paid no attention but kept walking steadily forward and they were soon out of sight.

One man was so sure that the mule was going to act up any minute that he followed them for several miles into the hills, but Lightning seemed to have found whatever it was looking for and never made a fuss at all. Neither the man nor Lightning was ever seen again.

There's not much to do here at Panama City but share stories and play cards while we wait for the ship to take us up to California. I have not yet seen the elephant, but I know it's just around the bend.

Take care of each other, my dears. Pet Rags for me and give Old Dorcas a carrot until I can do those things myself.

Until then,
I remain, your devoted father and husband,
Miles Corbin

"Read it again," said Rachel, breaking the silence that followed. "Do you think Lightning is all right?"

Robbie said, "I sure wish we had a mule like Lightning."

"A mule!" said their mother. She stood up. "That's just what we need, another useless animal to care for."

Sarah sighed. "His story was a good one, wasn't it?" She turned to her mother. "Wasn't it?"

"Stories," she said. "We hang by our toenails and he sends us stories." She left the room, shaking her head.

"Why is she mad, Sarah?" Rachel whispered, twisting her hair. "Didn't she like the letter?"

"She's just tired, Rache," Sarah said. "The important thing is, we've heard from Father and he's all right. Soon he'll be in California and he'll get the gold and come home again. It's time for supper. Let's get washed up."

"Mother?" Sarah asked later as she entered the kitchen, where her mother stood at the stove stirring the stew. "Aren't you happy to hear from Father?"

"I'd have been happier to hear he'd turned 'round and was headed home."

"Without the gold?" asked Sarah.

"With the gold out of his system for good and for all." Mrs. Corbin began dishing out the stew.

"Sarah," Rachel said during supper, "will you read us the letter again?"

Sarah read them the letter after supper and again before they went to bed. Her mother went out on the porch.

After tucking Rachel and Robbie into bed, Sarah joined her mother. This was the part of the day she'd always loved best. She missed her father's song.

"You'll have to get your singing from the birds, I'm afraid," said her mother as if she had read Sarah's thoughts.

"Don't you miss him, Mother?"

"Miss him?" Her mother looked surprised. She stopped rocking and seemed about to say one thing and then changed her mind and began to rock again. "Sometimes," she admitted. "Most of the time I'm too tired and too busy to miss him."

"Is the work hard?"

"At the whip factory?" Of course she meant the whip factory. Why did her mother make every conversation so difficult?

"Yes, Mother, at the whip factory."

"No. Not really hard. Just long and dirty and noisy."

"What do you do there?"

"I braid cord around the whip handles and pass them on to be varnished."

"Is it the cord that cuts your hands?"

Her mother looked down at her bruised fingers. "Yes, sometimes the cord cuts my hands." She turned them over in her lap, then pulled her apron around them.

"Are the people there nice?"

"Nice? Nice enough, I guess. We don't get much time to talk. Time for bed." Her mother stood and went into the house. For a while Sarah stayed on the steps, listening to the song of the thrush.

6

Memories and News

"Why don't we make a scrapbook for Father?" Robbie asked one evening when the washing up was done. "We can use Rachel's book."

"The one Grandfather gave me for my birthday?" Rachel's lip quivered. It was a beautiful scrapbook, embossed leather with a bouquet of flowers in the center of the cover.

"Why not?" he said. "You never use it."

"I put my drawing of a cat in it."

"But there are all those empty pages. We can put all Father's letters in. We can put something in the scrapbook from each of us every day and then, when he comes back, he'll know the things we did while he was gone," Robbie said.

"Are you saving it for something special, Rachel?" Sarah asked.

"No," she said. "Not really." Rachel took the scrapbook down from the shelf and rubbed her hand over the cover. "Could we put pressed flowers in it? Father loves wildflowers. I could put in Johnny-jump-ups, and mayflowers and . . ."

"Too bad we can't put in bird songs," said Robbie. "Remember how Father would sit on the steps and whistle back at the thrush?"

"He could talk to the owls too, couldn't he?" Rachel's question was tentative.

Sarah smiled, remembering those winter evenings. They'd stood on the porch for what seemed like hours, listening for the owl's answer to their father's call. "That's right, Rachel."

"I thought so, but sometimes I think I just dreamt it. All right, we can use the scrapbook." She handed it to Robbie and grinned. "But my name stays on the first page."

So the nightly ritual began. After supper and chores, Miles Corbin's children would decide what would go in the scrapbook and whose turn it would be to secure each item on the page with flour and water paste. It seemed to bring their father closer somehow.

"What would you like to put in, Mother," Rachel asked the first evening, "to show Father about your day?"

"Put in a sore back and a torn shirtwaist," her mother said grimly.

Rachel looked from her mother to Sarah with a puzzled look.

Before she could speak, Sarah said, "Here, put in this tulip leaf."

She looked over at her mother, who sat, without further word, in the rocking chair in the corner of the room, darning and then nodding off until they all went up to bed.

The next evening the children were finishing up the dishes. Their mother was at the high spinning wheel in the front room when Hiram Beech knocked at the door. Robbie answered it.

Sarah smiled. She liked Hiram. They all did. "Rachel, go get Mother."

"Good evening, Hiram," Delina said as she entered the kitchen.

"Evening, Mrs. Corbin. Understand you're looking for a hired man."

"I am indeed," she said. "You're available, then?"

"Yes, ma'am," he said. "Work's hard to come by, these days. I was pleased to hear you were looking."

"Not interested in factory work, I take it," Delina said as she motioned him to a seat at the kitchen table and sat down herself.

"No, ma'am," he said. "Farming's the only thing I know."

"Well," she said, "we've plenty of farming here to do, but I don't know if it's enough to support you till the crop comes in."

"Don't need much," he said. "There's just myself now."

Sarah knew he'd lost his wife and children to the

typhoid several years ago.

"I can pay you two dollars a week," her mother said, "plus meals, and there's a room in the back of the barn if you need one. And half of the produce. If the flax crop sells as I think it will, we should both end up with a bit of a profit."

"I get half of the flax, too?" he asked.

"Share and share alike with the profits. But I fear most of the work will fall on you," she said. "I'll supply the land and the seed and equipment." She smiled. "Done?"

"Done," he said. He stood up, grinning broadly at the children, who grinned cheerfully back. Having Hiram on the farm wouldn't make any difference with the housework, but it would surely mean fewer farm chores for them, and the problem of the flax was solved.

As they finished up the chores, Robbie began to sing, "It rained all night the day I left . . ."

In a moment Sarah and Rachel picked it up: "The weather it was dry. The sun so hot, I froze to death. Susanna, don't you cry."

As the many verses continued Sarah wasn't sure but she thought she heard her mother humming to the chorus: "Oh Susanna, Oh don't you cry for me."

The next letter came a few weeks later.

San Francisco, California
April 18, 1850
My Dear Delina and My Three Darlings,
Hope all is well in Westfield.

As you can see, I've arrived at last in California and nary a sight of Lightning, elephant, or gold yet.

After waiting a month in Panama, I took passage at last on the ship Daniel Webster *and arrived here without mishap although we were a sorry-looking lot when we disembarked. Not so sorry-looking as the folks that came across the plains though. One man I talked to had run out of water halfway through the desert and had to buy it from cutthroats who charged $100 a glass! Most people had to sell off just about everything they had, including the clothes on their backs, just to get here.*

California is a busy place. There is a lot to see and do but you were right not to come, Delina. This is no place for ladies. The women here are rough and tough as men. You have to plow your way through the crowds to buy anything and everything is priced for millionaires.

My stake ran out

"What!" Delina's voice broke in. "His stake ran out!"

Sarah went on quickly.

so I'm doing day work until I can get enough to head for the fields.

Sarah glanced quickly at her mother, but she sat tight-lipped with her arms across her chest.

At sixteen dollars a day, it shouldn't take long.

"Sixteen dollars a day!" Robbie exclaimed. "That's a lot, isn't it, Sarah?"

Sarah nodded, patted her brother's leg, and continued.

When I find my first gold, I'll have my likeness taken and send it back to you so you can see what I look like these days.

Sarah's eyes flew to her mother again, but there was no reaction.

I should have it better in the gold fields than most of these folks. At least I'm used to digging and carrying. Lots of people have stopped looking for gold and have set up businesses here supplying the ones still searching. They offer all kinds of gold digging supplies: devices that channel river water for panning, shovels, picks, and clothing, all for the most amazing prices. The gold is in the hills and in the rivers but it's hard to get at.

In a week I should have enough money and I'll head for the middle fork of the American River. They say the panning there is good.

More when I get back.

Hope all are well.
Your loving father and husband,
Miles Corbin

"There's no story," Rachel said when Sarah had finished reading it. "I wanted a story." Her lower lip trembled.

"I wish I was there," said Robbie. "I'm strong. I could carry the gold."

"I just want him to come home," said Sarah.

"He ran out of money," Delina said, more to herself than anyone else. "How could he have spent it all?"

"He can't help it!" Sarah rose to his defense this time. "Everything's expensive. He said so. Didn't you hear it? And he's going to make sixteen dollars a day. That's a lot!"

Her mother looked at her sharply, then seemed to bite back the angry words. She sighed. "He can't help it. He never could." She shook her head and left the room.

Although they worked on the scrapbook that night with more vigor than usual, Rachel and Robbie didn't ask for the last letter to be read again. It was Sarah who read both letters every night before she went to sleep.

"Sarah," Rachel asked one night as they sat

around the table, each writing a note about their day for the scrapbook. "What does Father look like?"

"He's big and tall with dark brown eyes," Sarah said. "Don't you remember?"

"Sometimes I think I do, and sometimes I get him mixed up with Grandfather."

"Oh, he's not a bit like Grandfather," Robbie said decisively. "More like Mr. Evans, the blacksmith, only Father has lighter hair and a bump on his nose where it was broken."

"How did he break his nose?" Rachel asked and settled in for the story she knew was to come.

7

Grandfather's Reaction

Sarah was making soap on a hot July morning. She wished she could wait for a cooler day, but the cracklings would spoil if they weren't used soon. Last night she and her mother had taken them from the cellar and heated them in the big kettle on the stove. Now Sarah sprinkled the fat with lye and added water, taking out flecks of meat as they boiled to the top. She put down the long spoon and went to answer a knock at the door.

"Grandfather!" she said with surprise. He seldom came to the farm, although his home was only a mile or two away.

He carried his cane in one hand, and under the other arm he held a large ball. He turned and rolled it out into the yard. "Thought the children might need a new one," he said, nodding in the direction of the ball.

"Thank you, Grandfather," she said. "Robbie and Rachel will love it."

"I've missed you, Sarah. Why haven't you come to see me?"

She had to think for a moment. She did usually manage to visit her grandfather every few weeks. He lived only a mile or so away, and Sarah always enjoyed the visits to his big house on Broad Street. Lately, though, everybody had been working so hard nobody had thought of being social.

"Just too busy, I guess," she said. "I'm sorry. Won't you come in, Grandfather?"

"Why are you not at school?" he said, turning as he stood on the porch to look around him. Sarah could tell he was not pleased with what he saw. They'd been working as hard as they could, but she knew some things had been let go. Hiram had been too busy plowing and planting to get very far on repairs and upkeep. A quick glance around showed her that the barn door could use a coat of paint and the step into the milk room was split and tipped.

Still, Sarah thought, they hadn't done all that badly. The rows in the garden might not be straight, but they had already yielded beans, peas, and spinach. The tomatoes had set and were nearly ripe. She and her mother had put up some of the beans for next winter. The flax was growing in the field and should bring a good harvest. Paint and steps and other repairs could wait.

"Rachel and Robbie are there now," she said, hoping he wouldn't notice that she'd dodged the question. She might have known better.

"You ought to be with them," he said.

"Too much to do here. I'll go back after harvest

when the next session starts up," she said. "I'll catch
up quickly."

"You should be getting more schooling, Sarah."

"Our school's a small one, Grandfather. It can't
afford to be open as much as the bigger schools are."

"Where is your mother, child?"

To give herself time to compose an answer, Sarah
headed for the kitchen. He followed, pulled back a
chair, and sat at the table. She stirred the soap again
and held up the spoon. The mixture coated it with a
creamy layer.

"Sarah," he said, with some impatience.

"Please excuse me, Grandfather," she said. "I've
got to finish this up and then we can talk." She
poured a spoonful onto a plate. To her great satisfac-
tion, it hardened just right, not too brittle and not
too soft. She started to lift the heavy kettle, but
Grandfather stood, pushing her away, and poured
the mixture into the galvanized tub himself.

"Thank you! That was heavy," Sarah said, wiping
her forehead with her sleeve. Her shirtwaist clung to
her back. She knew it was drenched with sweat.
Looking down, she could see the dampness leaking
through her shirtwaist around her underarms. She
knew she looked a mess, but this was the first time
she'd completed the entire process of making soap on
her own. She felt quite proud of herself.

"Where is your mother?" Grandfather asked again as she sat opposite him at the table. "Why is my granddaughter doing the chores of a scullery maid?"

"Mother is at the factory," Sarah said tentatively, answering his first question, as the second one seemed impossible.

His eyebrows went up. "What factory?"

Sarah closed her eyes. She hated to go on, but there was nothing for it. She looked straight at him and delivered the blow. "Mother is working at the whip factory, Grandfather."

"No!" Sarah jumped as he slammed his walking stick down on the table so hard Sarah feared either the table or the stick would break, but neither one did. Sarah stood her ground. She had learned that it never did to show fear to her grandfather.

She said quietly, "We use the money she makes there to hire Hiram Beech to plant and harvest the flax."

"And your father?"

Sarah took a deep breath. "My father is in the gold fields, as you well know, Grandfather."

For a moment, his eyes flared. "Watch your tongue, Sarah," he said. He shifted in his chair. "He's been gone, what? A year?"

"Six months," she said. Actually, it had been a bit longer than that.

"And I suppose you hear from him often?"

"Yes," she said.

"How many letters?" he persisted.

"Two," she said. She couldn't lie to him.

He looked disgusted. "No word since when?"

"April," she said.

"April," he repeated, nodding his head.

"Well, he wrote it in April but we didn't get it until June. That's not so very long, Grandfather. He writes when he can and the letters take a long time to get here."

"I'm sure." But it didn't look as though he meant it. He looked around the kitchen with disdain. "My only daughter works in a factory. Her husband is off on a lark while my granddaughter . . ."

"Keeps things going here," Sarah finished before he could supply other words.

He shook his head. "I had hoped my grandchildren would be raised properly. Instead my daughter marries a man who neglects his family for a wild goose chase."

Sarah stood up quickly and grasped the edge of the table for support. "He doesn't neglect us! It isn't a wild goose chase! There is gold in California and he's bringing it home and then we'll have the life you're talking about. You'll see!"

"We'll all see, shan't we?" he said grimly. They

glared at each other in silence for a while before Sarah released her grip and sat back down.

"What time does your mother get home?"

"Suppertime," Sarah said. Her face felt hot; she could feel the pulse in her cheeks. She went over to the basin and splashed her face with water.

"And when is suppertime?" he asked.

"Around six-thirty," she said, turning back from the basin.

"Tell her to come to see me." Grandfather stood up.

"I'll tell her that you want to see her, but I doubt she'll go. She's usually too tired to go anywhere."

"Then I shall come back," he said, taking up his hat and cane. "Sarah." He turned to face her. His voice was soft. "You don't have to do this. Just because my daughter is a fool doesn't mean that you must be one too."

"Mother is not a fool. She works hard. She's a good mother!"

Sarah could hardly believe she'd said that. She was not at all sure she believed it. Still, she couldn't allow Grandfather to say such things.

"Sarah," he said, even more gently, "come and live with me. You know I can give you the best. This is no work for you."

"Live with you?" Sarah's mind flew in many

directions. She was needed here. If she left, who would do the housework? Live with Grandfather! It was impossible.

Grandfather's house was wonderful. It dominated Broad Street, with its red brick and creamy white woodwork trim, bigger and more beautiful than its elegant neighbors. Sarah loved the front portico that stretched up two floors and the fanlight that topped the double doors. Two large columns framed the doorway, and a large wrought-iron lantern hung down on a long chain from the second-floor level. Sarah always felt like a fine lady when she reached up to the brass knocker.

Sarah shook her head as the thoughts flew through her mind. Live with Grandfather. What a thought! He was fun to visit and she was always glad when he came to the farm — well, except for this visit, perhaps. She'd never seen him dressed other than he was now — in a black, short coat and tan breeches. He wore a black satin vest that displayed his carefully polished gold watch fob perfectly. When she was little she had thought he slept in those clothes, for she couldn't imagine him in a nightshirt. His hair was snow white and always neatly trimmed and combed. He carried the gold-topped cane, but he seldom leaned on it.

"Would Rachel and Robbie come, too?" she asked.

"Of course," he said. "You're all welcome." He headed toward the door. "Think about it, Sarah, and tell your mother I'll be back."

Her mother greeted the news of her father's visit with a nod but said nothing as she went about dishing out the supper.

"Mother," Sarah said after Robbie and Rachel were in bed, "I was right to tell him, wasn't I? About your work, I mean."

"He had to find out sometime," her mother said. "I'd have thought some of the bosses at the factory would have told him the scandalous news by now."

"He doesn't like Father much, does he?"

There was a brief smile. "They have their differences."

"How can anybody not like Father?"

"Your grandfather has worked hard and enjoyed great success in the business world. He thinks your father should do the same."

"Maybe he can someday."

Her mother shook her head. "Your father is a dreamer and a storyteller, not a businessman." She stopped and looked straight ahead. Her face softened. "He couldn't be a businessman."

Sarah tried to picture her father dressed up in a top hat and formal clothes, and the image made her giggle. She couldn't erase her father's usual outfit of dark blue linen trousers and a loose shirt, his curly brown hair sticking up at the back no matter how he tried to keep it down.

"Do you suppose that when he gets home, Father will get himself a fancy walking stick like Grandfather's?" Sarah smiled broadly as she looked at her mother. For a moment there was the hint of a smile.

"I doubt very much if a walking stick is on his list of things to buy. Time for bed, Sarah."

8

News from the Gold Fields

Grandfather came back the next evening just as they were clearing the supper dishes. He rapped sharply on the door with his cane and then stepped inside.

"Good evening, Grandfather." Sarah, Rachel, and Robbie spoke in concert. The younger two were smiling broadly. Sarah's smile was more tentative. This, she knew, was not going to be an easy visit.

"Father," Mrs. Corbin said, wiping her hands on her apron. "Come in."

"I'm already in," he said.

"I know."

"Good evening, children," he said. He reached in his pocket and took out three horehound candies and handed one to each child. They murmured their thanks.

He looked at his daughter. "Want one, Delina?"

"No, thank you," she said.

"I need to speak with you, Delina."

Her mother nodded. Rachel and Robbie went outside, unwrapping their candies on the way. When Sarah moved to follow, her mother stopped her with a hand to her elbow.

"Stay, Sarah," she said. "This may concern you."

Sarah glanced quickly at her grandfather, who raised his eyebrows but said nothing as she cautiously joined them at the table. Her mother folded her hands on the tabletop, glanced down at them, and then quickly placed her hands in her lap as she faced her father.

"Has Sarah told you of my offer?" he asked.

Sarah spoke before her mother could. "There hasn't been time, Grandfather."

"I suppose you asked her to live with you," her mother said.

Sarah looked at her mother in surprise. How could she have known that?

"I did."

"And what was her answer?"

"She gave no answer," Mr. Wilcox said. "I suspect she needed time to think about it."

They spoke as if Sarah weren't there. She was about to say so when her mother turned to her.

"Have you thought about it, Sarah?" her mother asked.

"Some," she said. "But the pigs got out this morning and we had to spend so much time rounding them up that the rest of the work piled up and —"

"My granddaughter spent the day catching pigs." His face showed his disgust.

"Your granddaughter spent the day doing what

had to be done. She keeps this place going —"

"While you do the work of a mill girl," her grandfather interrupted.

"While I make enough money to hire help." Delina brushed away his words. "Thanks to Hiram the flax crop is a good one and the garden is doing well. Even with his split we'll have enough to keep us through the winter and pay off some of the debt."

He waved his hand in dismissal. "I can take care of the debt, Delina."

"No," she said, quietly. "No, Father, you cannot."

Looking nervously from one to the other, Sarah spoke before they could. "I'm needed here, Grandfather." There was pride in her voice. It was true. She was a necessary part of keeping things going on the farm while they waited for her father's return. "When my father comes back, we can pay off all the debt, Grandfather. Then there will be time to visit you any time I want." She smiled at them cheerfully, hoping to make everything all right between her mother and her grandfather.

Grandfather paused only a moment and then leaned across the table toward his daughter. "Have you heard lately from Miles?"

"You know that we have not."

"I have news of him," he said, "but not directly."

"Oh!" Sarah jumped up and ran to him. "What

news? Is he all right?" She tried and failed to read her grandfather's face as he stared at her mother.

"I've had a letter from the Otis boys," he said. "They saw Miles panning for gold on a branch of the American River not far from them."

"He got to the gold fields, then," her mother said.

"Apparently," he answered.

"Have the Otis boys found gold?" asked Sarah.

"They have."

"Then Father must be finding it, too." Sarah could hardly keep herself from jumping up and down. "He's done it. He's seeing the elephant and bringing home the gold!"

Grandfather looked confused. "There are no elephants in California."

Her mother smiled. "It's a long story."

"One of Miles's, no doubt." He smiled grimly, pausing a moment before continuing. "While it is true that Jess and Daniel Otis have found gold on that river, it does not necessarily follow that Miles has done the same. If he had found it, don't you think he'd have written?"

"Perhaps he's on his way back," her mother said.

"He is! I know he is!" Sarah exclaimed. How could her mother sit there so calmly?

"Father," Delina said, ignoring Sarah's outburst, "how is it that the Otis boys have written to you?

Their families would surely like such news."

"I have told their families their good news," he said.

"And no doubt they were pleased," Delina agreed. "But why did they write to you?"

"I have an interest in their journey," he said, shifting a bit in his chair.

"Ah," her mother nodded. She looked directly at her father. "You have an interest. You underwrote their expenses for a portion of the gold."

"I did."

"Miles —"

"Miles asked me for money, Delina, for this adventure like all the other ventures that were supposed to make him rich. This time I refused." He stood. "Sarah, I hope you will reconsider my offer."

"But I don't need to, now," she said. "My father will be back soon and we'll be rich."

"There's many a slip 'twixt the cup and the lip," her grandfather said. "Don't plan on anything where your father is concerned." He took up his hat and cane and closed the door softly behind him.

Robbie and Rachel came in as soon as their grandfather left. When they heard the news that their father had reached the gold fields, they jumped up and ran out into the yard with their whoops of joy. Sarah and her mother stood together on the porch, but Sarah smiled alone.

9

A Different View

A few days later, Sarah watched her grandfather come in at the front gate. There was a package tucked under his left arm.

She went out on the porch to greet him. It was another scorcher of a day.

"Good morning, Grandfather," she said. She searched his face for information.

"Good morning, Sarah."

"Mother is at work."

"No doubt," he said, handing her the package. "A little something."

"Thank you, Grandfather. What is it?" she asked. The box was about a foot long and neatly wrapped.

"A new invention I've an interest in. Just a toy, really," he said. "I thought it might amuse you all."

Sarah took out a strange device that seemed to be some sort of metal mask with a wooden handle on a hinge below it. A slat of wood stuck out from just below the mask. A metal rack slid back and forth along the slat. She turned it over in her hands, trying to make sense of it.

"What is it, Grandfather? What's it for?"

"They call it a stereoscope."

"How does it work?"

He took it from her and extended the handle. He picked up a cardboard strip on which were two identical images of a little dog. He put the strip in the rack, viewed it through the lenses and adjusted the rack. "Now," he said, "look through here." He handed it to Sarah.

Sarah put her face into the mask and squealed. A single picture sprang out at her as if it were real. The little dog seemed to be standing way out in front of the barn door. She reached out to touch the dog but found only the same two images. She looked back through the viewer again. "Oh," she said. "How does it do that?"

"Your eyes do it," Grandfather said. "It's quite simple, really. The two images look exactly alike, but one is taken with the camera a few inches over. When you look through the stereoscope, your eyes put the two images together and make the single picture appear to have depth. It's just a different view of things."

"This is wonderful. Robbie and Rachel are going to love it. Are there more pictures? Can I see them?"

"I'm glad you like it, Sarah." His smile was brief. "You can look at them all later."

Sarah smiled. "Thank you, Grandfather. I'm sure we'll all enjoy it."

He leaned toward her. "Sarah," he said softly. "I

have had further news about your father and thought you ought to hear it. I would wait until evening when your mother is home, but I will be leaving town this afternoon for a few days' business."

She carefully placed the stereoscope on the table and stayed where she was, facing away from him. This didn't sound like good news.

Grandfather touched her shoulder. "Sarah, Jess and Daniel Otis are back. They fell far short of the tons of gold they hoped to find, but they have certainly paid off all investments, including their own."

"And —" She turned to face him.

"And they last saw your father booking passage on the ship *Industry* heading for Boston by way of the Horn."

"Then he'll be home soon," she said. She didn't care how much gold he had found. She wanted him back. "This is good news, Grandfather. Wait till Mother hears that!" She wasn't at all sure she was right. A look at her grandfather's face told her she hadn't received all the information yet.

"That's as may be, Sarah," he said. "There is, however, a problem."

She nodded, afraid to speak — afraid to hear the rest.

"They tell me that ship he sailed on left before their own and docked at Boston last month."

For a moment she stood blinking, trying to make sense of it.

"Then he should be here soon," she said tentatively.

"Then he should have been here weeks ago," said her grandfather.

"I'm sure there's a reason."

"I'm sure there is," he said. "I'm just not sure that we'll like that reason. I'm sorry, Sarah. I wish I had better news."

She said nothing. Her mind was racing to think of a reason why her father wasn't home by now, but she could think of none.

She hardly noticed when, with a pat on her shoulder, Grandfather left.

Sarah spent the rest of the day in torment. What could be keeping her father? Why hadn't he rushed back to them? Fortunately, Rachel and Robbie were at school and wouldn't be home until four, so she didn't have to deal with them yet. Then perhaps the stereoscope would keep them busy when they did get home. She wasn't sure what, if anything, she should tell them. Better to let her mother decide. Sarah began cleaning and refilling the oil lamps with hands shaking so hard she nearly dropped a glass chimney. She put together a shepherd's pie for supper and paced the room while it cooked.

When they came in, Rachel and Robbie were too excited by the stereoscope to ask any questions other than "How does it work?" Once they found out, they had to view each picture in the deck before they started over.

Her mother stepped inside the door, glanced at Sarah, and stopped immediately. "What is it?" she said. "What's happened?"

"Look, Mother!" Rachel said. "See what Grandfather brought!"

"It's a stero . . . What is it, Sarah?"

"A stereoscope," Sarah said, her eyes on her mother.

"It's a stereoscope, Mother!" Rachel repeated. "Want to see?"

"Not right now," Delina said. "Why don't you go show it to Hiram? He's in the barn."

Grabbing all the equipment, Robbie followed Rachel out the door. Mrs. Corbin turned toward her daughter. "What is it?" she asked again.

Sarah's mouth opened but no words came out. Tears sprang to her eyes.

"Your father?" her mother asked, taking a step closer.

Sarah nodded as the tears ran faster.

"Dead?" Delina asked. She reached out a hand to steady herself on the chair.

Sarah stifled her tears as she shook her head. He wasn't dead. Of course he wasn't dead.

"No, not dead," she said, "but oh, Mother, he should be home and he isn't."

"Who says that he should?" Before Sarah could speak, Mrs. Corbin answered her own question. "My father," she said firmly. "And he brought the viewer."

Sarah nodded, taking a deep breath and brushing back her tears.

"Father's boat landed in Boston last month."

For a moment Delina just stared at her, absorbing the news. Then she nodded, turned, and walked to the rocking chair on the porch.

For a few more minutes Sarah cried. Then she splashed her face with water from the basin and went to join her mother on the porch. By this time, Robbie and Rachel had tired of the stereoscope and were walking along the top of the stone wall. Shouting and laughing, they tried to push each other off.

Her mother was rocking very fast, her feet making a rhythmic shuffle between the clicks and squeaks of the rocker. Except for the speed of rocking, there was no sign that her mother was upset.

For a while they sat in silence.

"There are lots of reasons why he might not be here yet," Sarah said.

Her mother nodded. "There are."

"He could have taken a different boat."

"He might have."

"He could have had trouble finding a way to Westfield." But she knew that didn't make sense. He could have walked to Westfield by now.

Her mother's raised eyebrow showed what she thought of that notion.

Sarah tried again. "Something must have happened to delay him."

Her mother nodded.

"He might have stopped to visit friends," Sarah said, although why he would do such a thing with his family waiting, she could not comprehend.

Her mother seemed to consider it. "I'm sure he'll be here soon."

"Perhaps," her mother said.

"Of course he will!" Sarah stood, facing her mother in her anger. "He will come back as soon as he can. He said he would. He loves us!"

"Perhaps he will be home soon, but we'll keep this latest information between the two of us, Sarah. There's no good in upsetting them." She nodded toward her younger children.

"You mean keep it between the three of us," said Sarah. "Don't forget Grandfather."

"No, Sarah," said her mother. "I shall not forget Grandfather."

10

Cuts and Bruises

The next Saturday it was Robbie again who brought home the letter, but he was not running and shouting. Instead, with a puzzled look on his face, he handed the envelope to Sarah. "Who would be writing to us from Boston?" he said, reading the return address.

"Why, I don't know." Sarah wiped her hands on her apron and took it. It was not her father's handwriting. Only the words "Boston, Massachusetts" were in the upper-left-hand corner of the envelope. The only name on the envelope was her mother's. As far as she knew, her mother knew no one in Boston. Perhaps it was news of her father. Perhaps some friend had seen him and written them about it. Perhaps he was ill and had to remain in Boston until he was well again.

She'd have thought about the letter longer if the pigs hadn't gotten loose again. Then, before Sarah had caught her breath, Rachel limped in screaming and holding her knee. Rags followed, barking loudly, and Robbie was not far behind. Blood ran down between Rachel's fingers, and she screamed louder as she came into the kitchen.

Grabbing a cloth from the sink, Sarah sat her

sister down in the chair and knelt in front of her.
Rachel refused to sit back and kept one arm around
Sarah's neck and the other on her knee as she
screamed and sobbed.

"What happened?" Sarah asked as she dabbed at
the blood running down Rachel's leg.

"I fell . . . out of the apple tree," Rachel sobbed
between hiccups. "I was . . . trying to reach the . . .
old robin's nest and I fell."

"She landed on a rock, Sarah," Robbie said excit-
edly. "She hit three branches on her way down."
There was admiration in his tone.

"Are you hurt anywhere else?" Sarah asked.

The little girl shook her head. "I don't think so,"
she said.

The dog sniffed at her knee, trying to lick the
blood.

"Let me see it," Sarah said.

"No! No! You'll hurt it!"

"You've already hurt it," Robbie said. "Let Sarah
see how bad it is. It's really awful," he told Sarah.

"No! Don't look at it! Don't touch it!" Rachel
grabbed the knee with both hands. Blood dripped
out between them.

"You'll bleed to death, then," Robbie said.

Rachel gasped. "Bleed to death? Am I going to
die?" she asked Sarah.

"No," she said. "You won't die, but something's got to be done with that knee."

"I want Mother to do it." Rachel was defiant.

"Well then, you'll have to wait a long time," Sarah said, looking at the clock. "This is Saturday, so Mother will be home early but not until the middle of the afternoon."

"And by that time, you'll bleed to death," Robbie said.

"Robbie, hush!" said Sarah. She turned to her sister. "Move your hands away, Rachel."

With a wary look Rachel slowly removed her hands and they all gazed at the long cut just below the knee.

"Yuck!" Robbie said. "That looks awful. They'll probably have to cut it off."

Rachel grabbed her knee again and howled.

"Robbie, take Rags and go down to the gate to wait for Mother."

"You said she wouldn't be home for hours!"

"Right!" said Sarah. "Go wait."

"Come on, Rags," he said. He left the room but not before one more remark: "Rachel, if they cut off your leg, you can have a cane like Grandfather's."

"Robbie!" Sarah's arms were around her screaming sister.

"I was just trying to make her feel better," he said.

He shook his head in disgust. "Girls!"

Sarah moistened the cloth in the basin and gently began to wash away the dirt and the blood from her sister's leg. For a bit it bled more, but Sarah pressed the cloth against the wound and the bleeding let up, as did Rachel's tears. Sarah wrapped a strip of clean cloth around the wound and tied it.

"There!" she said. "That should hold it until Mother comes home. Let's get some of these wildflowers ready for the scrapbook."

The rest of the day passed peacefully enough, as they pressed flowers in the pages of the Bible. Whenever she remembered it, Rachel would look at her bandage and her lower lip would tremble. Sarah distracted her but was unable to get any work done. Whenever she made a move to do something else, Rachel would cry and beg her not to leave.

Robbie came in and, after looking at the bandage, announced, "Shucks! The bleeding's stopped."

"It has?" asked Rachel.

"Unless . . . ," he said hopefully, "unless it's all just dammed up behind that bandage and, when you take it off, the blood will all gush out! That'd be great!"

Banished from the house again, Robbie waited at the gate until his mother came home.

"— and Sarah fixed it but it could still get infected, couldn't it?" he asked hopefully as he and his mother opened the door.

"How's the patient?" Delina asked.

"Mother!" Rachel nearly jumped up and then remembered her knee. She grabbed it and began to cry. "I hurt my knee," she said.

"How bad is it?" Mrs. Corbin asked over her shoulder as she bent over her younger daughter.

"I don't know. I cleaned it. I didn't know anything else to do." Still, Sarah felt pretty good about handling it all. She hadn't panicked. She hadn't been sick, even though the sight of all that blood had turned her stomach.

Carefully, her mother removed the bandage. It stuck lightly to the wound and Rachel yelped. Paying no attention to that, Mrs. Corbin examined the knee, gently touching it around the edges.

"Ouch! Don't touch it!" Rachel yelled.

A look from her mother stopped Rachel from pulling away. Mrs. Corbin bandaged the wound with a clean cloth strip.

"Looks all right to me," she said. "No more climbing trees for you, young lady, at least not until that knee heals."

She turned to Sarah and gave a quick nod. Sarah waited for more. A comment about how well she had done would have been nice, but Mrs. Corbin began dishing out the supper without another word.

Supper was nearly over before Sarah remembered the letter. "Mother," she said, "this came today. Maybe it's about Father."

She handed it to her mother, who looked over the envelope carefully before breaking the seal. She began to read it aloud.

My Dear Mrs. Corbin,
It is with deep regret that I inform you of the tragic death of your . . ."

She read no further but reached out for her children.

Later, Rachel brought the scrapbook out. "What shall we put in it tonight?" she asked and seemed puzzled when everybody's tears started afresh. "Oh," she said, remembering, "it was for Father, wasn't it?" She carefully placed the scrapbook on the shelf, her hand stroking the cover as she did so.

11

He's Gone

It was late in the evening before they read the rest of the letter, and it was Robbie who asked for it. "How did Father die?"

Mrs. Corbin picked up the letter. She took a deep breath and then began to read:

It is with deep regret that I inform you of the tragic death of your husband, Miles Corbin. The breath Sarah drew was in concert with her mother's. *He was aboard the good ship* Industry *as we made our way back to Boston and, through misadventure or design, went overboard off Cape Horn on May 22, this year of our lord, eighteen hundred and fifty.*

"Overboard!" Robbie said. "Into the ocean?" Another thought struck him. "What does 'by design' mean?"

"It means on purpose," his mother said.

"On purpose? Why would he drown on purpose?"

"Did Father drown?" Rachel asked.

Her mother nodded and then read on.

A small trunk containing some of his things can be obtained at the address below or will be sent to you

upon written request.
   My sincere sympathy to you and your family.
   I remain,
   Josiah Trumbull, Ship's Captain
   The Industry
   32 Newbery Street
   Boston, Massachusetts

Sarah sat with her head in her hands. How awful it must have been for her father to die so far away from home in that cold, cold sea. She pictured him thrown about by the waves, calling for help. A more hopeful thought occurred to her then: her father was a strong swimmer. Could he have swum to land? In some of Grandfather's books there were stories about shipwrecked sailors who'd survived at sea. She knew it was unlikely that he could have made it, but it was possible.

She looked up at her mother, who sat with her head down, holding the letter.

"Why is the captain so sure Father is dead?" Sarah asked.

Her mother shook her head. "I don't know."

"He can't know it for sure, can he? All he knows is that Father went overboard. That doesn't necessarily mean he's dead. He could have swum to land or been picked up by another boat. Father's a strong swimmer. Remember how he swam the whole length of Congamond Middle Lake? Couldn't he have made it?"

"The captain must know, Sarah. He says it quite clearly."

"Did someone throw him overboard?" Robbie asked. "Could that be the design?"

"Maybe," Sarah said. She looked at her mother. "He was coming home with gold. Maybe Robbie's right. Maybe somebody did steal his gold and throw him overboard."

"As for that," Mrs. Corbin said, "we'll never know." She sat up straighter in her chair.

"Is the gold gone?" Rachel asked.

"Yes," said her mother. "There'll be no more talk of gold."

That night, Rachel and Robbie slept in their mother's bed. Sarah lay in her own, trying to stifle her sobs.

12

Mourning

Neighbors, hearing the dreadful news, came to the farm the next morning with dishes of food and words of comfort. Most of them clustered around Mrs. Corbin. Some cried. Others talked softly. Some of the women urged food on the children. Sarah couldn't eat. She couldn't even stop the shaking that seemed to take over her body. Rachel and Robbie were delighted with so many choices of good things to eat. They filled their plates and went outside with their friends.

Grandfather was among the first to arrive. When his daughter stood to greet him, he reached out as if to hug her but then seemed to reconsider and patted her upper arm awkwardly. He spoke softly to her and then turned to Sarah.

"My dear," he said, "I'm so very sorry."

Sarah fell into the comfort of his arms and sobbed.

"There, there," he said softly, patting her back as he held her.

"You didn't even like him," Sarah said as she recovered a bit and drew back.

"Your father and I had our differences, but we loved the same people," he said. "There was much to admire in Miles Corbin."

As the day went on, people came and went but Grandfather stayed on. He had brought more pictures for the stereoscope, and that occupied Rachel and Robbie when they were too full to eat any more.

In the evening he played checkers with Robbie and Rachel, taking them both on at once. Sarah sat on the settee watching them, but almost immediately her eyes grew heavy and she knew nothing more until morning, when she woke up in her own bed.

The mechanics of life didn't change much in the succeeding days. Her mother seemed to absorb the terrible news more easily than Sarah did. Their father had been gone so long that Rachel and Robbie, too, seemed to accept his permanent absence. Mrs. Corbin went back to work the next Monday morning.

"Don't you even care?" Sarah confronted her in the kitchen as her mother got ready to leave one morning.

Her mother turned and stared at her.

"I care," she said.

"You act as though nothing had happened. He's gone! Father's dead!"

"I know very well that he is dead," her mother said. "Do not make the mistake of thinking the person who cries the loudest cares the most."

Delina Corbin left, closing the door behind her.

13

Fire

Sarah was baking bread on a Saturday morning several weeks later. Hiram had gone to town for supplies, and she hoped to have the bread ready by the time he got back. It was the household job she liked best, and one of the few chores she did that didn't somehow remind her of her father. Well, not much anyway.

She loved each careful step: getting the fire in the stove just right, putting yeast, sugar, and a small amount of flour in warm water to form the sponge, watching it bubble, then adding more flour and kneading the dough. She liked the kneading best, squeezing the soft, warm dough beneath her fingers, letting go, and then squeezing again. After that there was the rest time, with the loaves sitting in cloth-covered pans until they doubled in size. Another kneading and another rise, and the loaves were ready for baking. The smell was the best smell ever, she decided, proud that her bread these days was almost as fine as her mother's. Robbie and Rachel didn't even complain about it anymore. If her mother noticed the gradual improvement, she didn't say so. On the other hand, she hadn't complained when Sarah's bread was coarse and hard, either.

Sarah had heard rumbles of thunder all morning and was aware now that the claps were closer and louder. She heard the rain come as one particularly loud boom shook the ground. She went to the door to summon Robbie and Rachel, but they were nowhere in sight. She hoped they'd taken shelter in the barn. She peered in that direction but the rain was coming down so hard, she couldn't see much.

She was back at the bread when she heard Rachel screaming.

"Come! Sarah, come!" Rachel yelled as she came in the door. Her arms were flailing wildly. "Fire!"

She grabbed Sarah's hand and, without pause, ran back with her to the barn. Rags was barking loudly, running back and forth in front of the barn doors, one of which was slightly ajar. Rachel pointed at the barn, jumping up and down yelling, "Stop it! Stop it!"

Flames licked out of the side window.

"Is Robbie in there?" Sarah asked.

Rachel just screamed, "Stop it, Sarah! Oh, please! Stop it!"

Sarah grabbed Rachel by both shoulders. "Where's Robbie?" Rachel pointed at the barn. Sarah could hear Dorcas neighing and kicking at his stall.

"Go get help!" Rachel seemed frozen in place. Sarah shook her again. "Rachel, now! Go to the

Strongs'! Go get help!"

"Get Robbie!" Rachel yelled.

"I'll get Robbie," Sarah yelled back at her. "Go get help, Rachel! Go now!"

Rachel ran down the road toward the Strongs'.

Sarah opened the big barn door. Smoke billowed out. She choked and stepped back, then dashed inside. The fresh air gave the fire inside a burst of new energy, and flames shot up against the nearest wall. Sarah ran to the smoldering left wall. Immediately, heavy smoke engulfed her. She drew her apron up over her nose and mouth. The heat was overpowering. "Robbie!" she coughed. "Robbie, where are you?"

Unable to see more than a foot or so ahead, Sarah followed the sounds of Dorcas's banging against the stable door as she worked her way along the wall toward the stall.

The smoke was heavy here, but at least the flames had not yet reached it. Sarah's eyes burned and every breath seared her lungs. As she approached the stall door, she tripped.

She stopped the fall against the stall door and looked down. Robbie was lying face down on the floor. "Robbie!" she cried. The shirt on his back was on fire. She smothered each flame with her hands, not even aware of the pain. Robbie didn't move.

She grabbed him around the waist, wincing now at the pain in her hands, and pulled and dragged him into the stall, slamming the double door shut with her hip. There was less smoke in here and no flames as yet, but she knew she didn't have much time. The horse reared up, its front hooves pawing the air, his eyes rolled back with fright. She had to get them out of here, but Robbie was too heavy for her to carry him to safety.

"It's all right, Dorcas," she said, speaking as calmly as she could. She put her hands up to stroke his neck. That hurt, so she drew back, but even that slight touch seemed to calm the horse a bit. She rubbed her shoulder against him as Dorcas brought his legs down. The whites of his eyes were showing and his skin quivered.

Sarah grabbed his water bucket with her wrists and threw the contents against the door and inside wall. It wouldn't help for long. They couldn't stay there, however much she was tempted. The hay in the barn must have caught by now. Soon even this place would be in flames and they'd be trapped.

She tried to grab Robbie to lift him onto Dorcas's back and screamed with the pain. She tried using her wrists to lift him, but she lacked the strength to get him high enough. Looking wildly around for a halfway point, she opened the top half of the stable door, letting in clouds of smoke. Some of the rafters had caught. Coughing and choking, she hoisted Robbie up onto the stable half door and turned to the horse.

Gingerly, she grasped the bit. Sometimes Dorcas fought it, but not today, thank goodness. He took the bit quickly and Sarah threw a blanket over his back. She led him up against the stable door. The horse pulled away from the heat, but years of obedience overcame his fear. Twisting the reins around her upper arms so that the horse could not retreat, Sarah stepped up on a stool and, using all her strength and will, lifted Robbie's unconscious body from the door onto Dorcas's back. She pulled from the other side until the load was balanced.

"Come, boy," she said softly and opened the bottom half of the door, leading the horse through with its precious burden.

Flames were overhead now as the fire in the rafters spread. For a moment Dorcas followed, but he stopped when he saw the wall of fire in front of them. Before he could rear up again, Sarah untied her apron and put it over the horse's face. She tugged the blanket out from under Robbie and laid it down over the flames. They lessened a bit, and she urged the horse slowly forward. "Come on, boy," she pleaded, trying to keep her voice calm. "Good boy, Dorcas."

Unable to see the flames, the horse followed hesi-
tantly.

Flames licked at her skirt, and it smoldered but did
not catch. The horse whimpered and tried to pull
back, but her grip was firm.

"Come, boy. Come," she said. At last they reached
the big outside door. Sarah stumbled outside into the
precious cooling rain. Gasping in deep breaths of
fresh air, she was barely aware of the people there.
She recognized Hiram rushing toward her as she fell
to the ground.

She came to in her own bed. She lay still for a
moment, unsure of where she was and how she had
come to be there. "Welcome back," said her mother.

In a flash Sarah remembered. "Robbie!" she said,
her voice a hoarse croak. "Where's Robbie?"

"At Grandfather's," her mother said. "He's got
some burns, and he was overcome by the smoke, but
he's going to be all right if pneumonia doesn't set in.
Have some broth."

Sarah was so relieved to think Robbie was all right
that another minute passed before she became aware
of the pain. In moments she was aware of little else.
Her hands were wrapped in moist bandages, but they
felt as if they were still on fire. She tried to move
them, only to scream with the pain. Her face hurt

almost as much as her hands. Every breath made her want to cry out. She tried to take small breaths.

"Just lie still," said her mother. "You've got some bad burns and you've scorched your lungs a bit, but the doctor says you'll be all right." She took a wet cloth, rubbed it with aloe, and dabbed at Sarah's face.

Sarah screamed at the touch.

"Let me," said her mother. "I know it hurts, but this will help." She touched Sarah's face more lightly this time. After the initial pain, the lotion felt cool and wonderful.

"Dorcas?" Sarah whispered.

"In the pasture now with the cows," said her mother. "The Strongs and Hiram are seeing to him. He's got a few burns, but he's fine."

"Rachel?"

"Our hero," said her mother. "She had sense enough to run to the Strongs' and get help. They couldn't save the barn, but they got the fire out before it spread to the house or the fields. The rain helped."

"I want to see Robbie." Sarah moved to sit up, but an agonizing pain enveloped her. It hurt too much to scream.

"Open your mouth," said her mother, moving a liquid-filled spoon toward her lips.

"What is it?"

"Laudanum. It will help the pain."

Gingerly, Sarah opened her lips and took the medicine.

"Hush now," said her mother. "There's nothing more for you to do now. Everything's fine. Shut your eyes and rest."

14

Recuperation and Relocation

During the long days and nights that followed, Sarah would wake from a drugged sleep to see her mother sitting beside her. Sarah's vision was often blurry, and she had trouble making out the other people who sometimes appeared in the room. Once she was sure it was her father. Other times the doctor or Grandfather stood by her bed. Several times it was Rachel who stood there. People said things, but Sarah seldom could understand what they said. Talking hurt too much to even try.

Often she thought she was still in the barn. There was fire all around her. She woke up gasping with fright and then pain.

At first the pain was so great and so constant that she scarcely noticed the intensified pain when the bandages were changed. The moist bandages, soaked in tea, had to be changed every day. The charred flesh would pull away with them, causing pain so great as to blot out everything else. As Sarah became more alert, more able to distinguish between the really bad pain and the times when it was lessened, the changing time became an occasion both Sarah and her mother dreaded. Even with a dose of laudanum first, it was impossible to accomplish the task without overwhelming, mind-shattering pain. After the first morning dose of the painkiller, Sarah would see her mother approaching with fresh bandages. She tried but couldn't stop the tears of fear and anticipation that sprang to her eyes.

"Nothing for it but to get it over with, Sarah," Mrs. Corbin would say as she unwrapped the bandages. "Try to think of something else."

That, of course, was impossible. Sarah would try, remembering riding Dorcas through the fields, while the first layers of bandages came off, but, as the layers unwound closer to her skin, the pain would overpower all thought.

Sometimes Sarah lost consciousness. She almost welcomed that, because she'd awake to find her hands in fresh bandages. Some days she fell asleep from the drug before her mother began, only to come to with a scream in the middle of the procedure.

Oh, how she wished her father were here. He'd have understood how awful the pain was. He'd have kept her from it — somehow. At least he'd have comforted her, sung to her, helped her get through it.

The doctor came frequently. Sarah knew he was coming when her mother took off the old bandages and didn't put on the new ones. In spite of the pain when the new bandages went on, Sarah hated this time, when her hands were uncovered. The air hurt.

Sarah never looked at her hands and arms when they were laid bare. She could imagine what they looked like. She didn't need to see them.

There were no bandages on her face. Sarah was afraid to ask, but one day she gathered her courage.

"My face," she began.

Delina had been about to leave the room. She stopped and turned back. "What about your face?"

"Is it awful?"

"I've always thought your nose was too short," her mother said. There was almost a smile.

"I mean the burns." Sarah was in no mood for joking.

"There are burns on your face."

"I know. But are they awful?"

"Look in the mirror and see for yourself." Her mother picked up the hand mirror.

Sarah turned away. "No! I can't," she said.

"They're not as bad as the ones on your hands and arms, Sarah. Take a look."

But Sarah turned away.

As the weeks went on, Sarah grew stronger. When the bandages had been changed, Delina would carefully lift her daughter into the chair, where she could sit a bit longer each day. It took several days before Sarah realized that the move was a bit less painful than it had been.

There was seldom a time when she was awake that her mother wasn't in the room, usually darning or knitting. Because the pain in Sarah's hands and on her face had lessened somewhat and her breathing was easier, she needed less laudanum each day. As her mind cleared, questions she'd been unable to form came to the surface.

"Robbie," she said to her mother one day. "Where's Robbie? Why won't you let me see him?"

"He's not here," her mother said. "He wasn't burned as badly as you, but he needed care — just not as much as you did. I couldn't care for you both. Your grandfather and the servants are doing for him. Robbie's not up to a trip here yet, and you're not in any condition to travel to him. You'll see him soon."

"Rachel must be lonely without him," Sarah said.

"Rachel is staying at Grandfather's as well. She comes over to see you whenever she can. She's having a great time. Both children are being spoiled rotten," said Delina.

Sarah was not at all sure she was getting the truth about Robbie. One day she waited until her mother had left the room before asking Rachel, "Is Robbie dead?"

"Dead?" Rachel looked confused. "No! He's not dead. But he might as well be. He sleeps most of the time. He's no fun at all."

Sarah looked up to see her mother in the doorway.

"I was afraid he was —," Sarah said.

"He's not dead, Sarah. You'll see him soon."

"He is going to be all right, isn't he? You said he was."

"Yes, Sarah. He's getting better. When you're well enough, we'll take you to see him."

"Have you seen him?"

"Oh, yes," she said. "Father and I switch places at night and I sit with Robbie for a bit. He's awake more and more. He asks about you all the time. He'll be all right. He's getting stronger."

One night Sarah woke up to see Grandfather sitting by the bed. He put down his book when he saw she was awake. He approached the bed, smiling broadly. "Do you need anything?" he asked.

"Water," she said.

He filled a glass from the pitcher and held it for her as she drank. As she sat back, he gently adjusted the blanket around her.

"How's Robbie?" Sarah asked.

"Doing splendidly," said her Grandfather. "Beats me at checkers every day."

He pulled his chair closer to her bed. "You were a very brave girl, my dear. Robbie owes you his life."

Tears sprang to her eyes. It was good to hear those

words. Father would have said them. She knew that. He'd be telling that story over and over again, celebrating her heroism to all within earshot. She grinned at the thought.

One day when the bandages had been changed and the agony was over for the day Sarah said, "I wish Father was here."

"If wishes were horses, beggars would ride," said her mother.

"I thought I saw him beside me when I was sick," she said.

"It was the laudanum. Sick as you were, you could have seen the devil himself," said her mother, grabbing up the dirty bandages as she left the room.

When Grandfather came by a day or so later, Sarah pumped him for news of Robbie. "He's sitting up and getting bored," he said. "He demands to be entertained. It keeps us all busy thinking of things to amuse him. I read to him often."

"Oh, I do miss reading," Sarah said. Actually, this was the first time she'd thought of it, but, now that she had, it seemed a big loss in her life.

"Nothing wrong with your eyes," Grandfather said. He grabbed a book from the nearby table and held it out to her. "Read, then."

She reached out her hands for it, and then drew them back as the hard surface met the tender flesh, even through the thick bandages.

"Well, then," he said, "let's try this." He opened the book and began to read. "*David Copperfield* by Charles Dickens. Chapter One. I Am Born."

For a while Sarah was caught up in the story, but very soon her eyes grew heavy. She was not aware when Grandfather left, leaving the book open on the table.

15

The House on Broad Street

One day Sarah awoke to hear her mother and grandfather talking softly outside her bedroom door.

"She's well enough now," he said. "Why put it off any longer? The children should be together."

"You're right," his daughter said. "It's time to bring Rachel and Robbie here."

"No, Delina. It's time to bring you and Sarah to them," he said. "There's no point in pretending it wouldn't be easier there. You've brought her through the worst of it, but she still needs care, and so does Robbie. And you need a full night's sleep."

"I can't just leave the farm," said her mother. "Miles —"

"Hiram can tend the farm. That's what you pay him for. Miles is dead," said Grandfather. "It's time to move on. Think about what's best for the children, Delina."

There was a long silence, and then she said, "I'll get the laudanum. She'll need it if we're going to move her."

Sarah sat up as her grandfather came in, followed by her mother, holding the spoon and bottle.

"You heard?" her mother asked.

Sarah nodded.

"All right?" Mrs. Corbin studied her daughter carefully.

Sarah was torn. She loved the farm, but staying with her grandfather sounded so good. Then she shook her head. "We mustn't leave the farm," she said.

"For now we must," said her mother. The decision was made. "We're not going far."

The laudanum did make what might have been a dreadful ride to Grandfather's house a hazy, almost painless one. Sarah was only dimly aware of being placed gently in the guest room she'd always liked best. As the laudanum wore off she could view the white on white embroidered bedspread, the rich, dark bedstead and chest of drawers, and the circular blue rug. Over the fireplace was a large portrait of a young man and woman, her grandmother and grandfather at the time of their marriage. She'd never known her grandmother and wondered what she had been like. If she gazed at the portrait through half-closed eyes, she could almost see her mother in that smiling face. Pleased at the new view, Sarah drifted off again, gazing at the portrait.

The next morning Sarah demanded to see Robbie, and one of the servants carried him into her room. He seemed small and very frail. His face was pale, but he smiled broadly and said, "Hey, Sarah. You haven't any eyebrows."

Grandfather grunted and then coughed to cover a laugh.

Mrs. Corbin said, "I think that will do it for today. You can see each other tomorrow," and Robbie was taken away.

"I thought you said they were growing back," Sarah accused her mother when the others had left.

"I did and they are," said her mother. She picked up a silver hand mirror and held it in front of her daughter's face, but Sarah had closed her eyes. "Look at yourself, Sarah," said her mother. "It's nowhere near as bad as you think it is."

Sarah shook her head and turned away.

"Yes," said her mother firmly. "Look now."

Her tone made it clear that she would not allow Sarah to avoid it this time. Slowly Sarah opened her eyes to see herself for the first time since the fire. Her face did look kind of funny, but it was not monstrous. Still, she thought with a smile, it was no wonder Robbie had thought she looked funny. There was just the suggestion of an eyebrow over each eye and a tiny brush of hair on her eyelids. There was a bald spot at the top of her forehead. Her face was red but, to her relief, there was only one spot near her ear where the skin looked raw and tight.

"It's looking better every day," Grandfather said.

He was standing in the doorway.

"Good as new in no time," said her mother. "Now your hands, Sarah."

Sarah drew them back. "The bandages —"

"I'll unwrap them," Mrs. Corbin said.

"No, I — I'll look tomorrow morning."

"No time like the present." Delina unwrapped the bandages. There was almost no pain.

"Look at your hands, Sarah."

"No," Sarah said.

Grandfather walked over to the bed. "Perhaps tomorrow would be better, Delina. She's had enough."

Delina shook her head. "I'll handle this, Father." She turned back to her daughter. "Look at your hands, Sarah. It's better to know."

Sarah slowly looked down. She drew in a sharp breath and tears filled her eyes as she saw through them to the damage. Angry, red scars covered every inch of skin on her hands and most of her forearms, one reaching up to the elbow on her right arm.

She looked up at her mother.

"Now," Delina said. "That's the worst of it. They're healing. They look lots better than they did. They'll look better yet."

Sarah nodded slowly. Her hands were monster hands. She knew they'd never look right again. She'd have to keep them hidden for the rest of her life. She couldn't speak as her mother put the bandages back on.

In the days that followed, Robbie and Sarah were brought downstairs often. It seemed a wonderful thing to Sarah after the long days alone with her mother at the farm to have people around, ready to talk, to read, to play games or fetch anything she wanted. She saw less of her mother and more of Grandfather, Rachel, and Robbie. Robbie seemed nearly back to his old self.

Early each morning, her mother came to change the bandages while Sarah was still in bed. Her grandfather had offered to do it, but it was Delina who came each morning. Sarah was just as glad. Her mother worked quickly and there wasn't as much pain now, but she wished she could sleep a bit later.

"Can't we do this later, Mother?" she asked one particularly sleepy morning.

"Not if I'm to do it," Delina said. "I've got to be to work in an hour."

"At the whip factory?" Sarah had assumed that her mother had quit the job.

"At the whip factory," her mother said. "You don't need me here every minute anymore. Robbie's nearly well and we still have debts to pay."

"What does Grandfather think about that?"

Delina smiled. "Oh, he's had his say."

Sarah smiled too, thinking of the arguments that must have filled the air.

After the mill closed on Saturdays, Sarah learned, Delina went to the farm to see to things and manage the accounts.

Anxious to keep her connection to the farm, Sarah quizzed her mother frequently. How was Rags? Was Dorcas being fed and exercised? What about the flax? Delina answered each question patiently.

There wasn't much Sarah could do with her hands yet. They hurt, but she wasn't taking any laudanum at all now. She still avoided looking at her hands when the bandages were off. They felt stiff and strange, and moving them hurt a lot.

Fortunately, there was much to occupy her mind in the big house on Broad Street. She had to have help bathing, combing her hair, dressing, and undressing, but she could come down the stairs by herself now, moving slowly and leaning her body hard against the strong oak railing. After resting a bit, she could then walk around the rooms. There was always a nearby chair to sit in when she felt weak or dizzy.

Her favorite place was the library, with its dark bookshelves reaching from floor to ceiling, with only the secretary desk to interrupt the walls of books that surrounded her.

Sarah often paused at the windowsill in the library to look at the white and pale green porcelain figurine of a handsome couple there. A man stood by a woman as she looked through a telescope. One of his hands held the telescope for her while the other gloved hand rested lightly on her shoulder. She imagined what they might be viewing through the scope. Birds, perhaps. One of the lady's snow-white hands gently touched the scope while the other, fingers slightly curled, lay gracefully on her lap. Such beautiful hands! Sarah thought of her own with their dreadful red scars. The thought made her turn away.

Another object that often captured her attention in the library was the large globe that stood in the corner. Rachel had to be cautioned against spinning it too hard, but Sarah would study the names and places on it, moving herself around since she couldn't yet bear to turn it with her hands.

There seemed to be more toys in the big house on Broad Street than Sarah had noticed before — hoops, dolls, and balls appeared on low shelves in the summer kitchen. Rachel had made friends with the little girl next door and so was never at a loss for something and someone to play with.

Grandfather read to them often. They had finished *David Copperfield* and were well into *Oliver Twist*.

One late afternoon Sarah and Robbie were in the

library with Grandfather. They'd been companion-
ably seated in big armchairs in front of the fire,
Grandfather reading. When Robbie fell asleep,
Grandfather put down the book.

Sarah wandered over to the globe and gingerly
touched its surface. Finding it only slightly painful,
she traced her father's trip down from Boston, across
the Isthmus, and up the coast of California. Her hand
moved to San Francisco and back down to Cape
Horn. There she stopped. She stared at the large
space of blue and choked back a sob. She looked up
to see her grandfather watching her.

Wordlessly, she shook her head and he nodded.
"We all miss him, Sarah."

"Mother doesn't," said Sarah.

"Of course she does," said Grandfather.

"Why doesn't she say so?"

"She doesn't need to."

"Why can't she be like other people?"

"In what way?" he asked. "Whom do you want
her to be like, Sarah?"

"I want her to talk to me. I want her to say nice
things. Why can't she smile and laugh? Why can't she
love us?"

"Of course she loves you. You, of all people, ought
to know she loves you, Sarah. She was with you
almost constantly after the fire."

"She never says so."

"Did your father love you?"

"Of course he does — did. He told us so."

"What if he didn't say so? Would you still know he loved you?"

"Yes," she said decisively.

"How?" he asked.

"He hugged us and he told us stories and he made us laugh."

"Do I love you?" Her grandfather was smiling now.

"Yes." She grinned.

"How do you know?"

"You're good to us. You read and talk and listen, but Mother's different."

"Step a few inches over, Sarah, and take a closer look at your mother," he said.

16

Facing Things

One early morning when her mother removed the bandages, Sarah waited for her to put new ones on. Instead, Delina bustled about the room, straightening things on the bureau.

"Is the doctor coming?" Sarah asked. He hadn't been by for several weeks.

"No," said her mother. "Your hands are better. You don't need the bandages anymore."

Sarah gulped. It was good to know she was better, but without the bandages to cover them people would see her hands. So would she.

"Look at them," said her mother.

"I did look at them," Sarah said. "They look awful!"

"They look better," said her mother. "Look at them."

Sarah looked down. The scars were still there — shiny raised places covering most of her hands and arms — but they did look pinker, less red and angry.

"It's time to get them working again," Delina said. She placed a ball of yarn in Sarah's right hand. "Squeeze it," she said.

"I can't."

"You can. Squeeze it."

Slowly, Sarah curled her fingers up until her fingertips touched it. She drew in her breath sharply.

"Squeeze," Delina said.

"It hurts!"

"Squeeze."

Sarah stared at her mother's determined face while her fingers closed down on the ball. The skin felt so tight that Sarah was sure it was splitting apart. She squeezed only a little and then dropped back.

"Other hand," said her mother.

Ignoring the tears that ran down Sarah's face, her mother changed the ball to the other hand. Sarah squeezed the ball.

"Enough," said her mother. "Let's get you dressed."

"What about my hands?" said Sarah.

"What about them?"

"People will see them."

"They will."

"Please put the bandages back on, Mother."

"You don't need them. If you don't start using those hands soon, they'll be useless. You'll never be able to use them."

"The scars —"

"The scars are there," her mother said firmly. "We'll soon get them working again, scars and all."

Sarah moaned and put her hands back under the

covers. Tears streamed down her face as she turned toward her mother. "They look awful."

"They look burned."

"You hide your hands because of the factory scars," said Sarah accusingly.

Her mother nodded. "So I do," she said, "but I shall do it no longer. Now, get up so I can help you dress or I'll be late for work."

After her mother left, Sarah stayed in her room. Later she grew bored and came downstairs, dreading the reaction of the others.

Rachel was the first to notice that the bandages were off. She ran over to Sarah.

"Let me see," she demanded. She looked but didn't touch them. "Do they hurt?" she asked.

"Not much anymore," Sarah said.

"Good," said Rachel, and she went outside to play.

Robbie looked carefully at Sarah's hands and even knelt down on the floor to look at them from beneath. Grandfather watched him warily.

"Wow!" Robbie said admiringly. "Can you move them?"

"Some," she said, and flexed her fingers a bit.

"Wow!" Robbie said again. "Burn scars look different from cut scars. I've got some on my back but I can't see them. The only one I can see on my arm isn't near as good as yours." He pulled back his sleeve to show a long burn scar on his forearm.

Sarah smiled. "That's right," she said. "Mine are better."

Robbie took another scone from the table and started out the door. He turned and came back to Sarah.

"I'm sorry," he said.

"What for?"

"For the fire. For your hurt hands."

"You didn't cause the fire," she said. "Lightning did. It's not your fault."

"If I hadn't been in the barn . . ."

"You might have been struck by lightning," said Sarah. "It's all right, Robbie. It wasn't your fault."

"Thank you for bringing me out," he said.

Sarah grinned. "I needed someone to play checkers with."

As they walked into the library, Grandfather glanced at her hands and smiled. "Worth a few scars for that, wasn't it?"

Sarah smiled tentatively. She wasn't so sure of that.

"They're looking better," he said.

"They look awful," Sarah said, her eyes full of tears.

"Give it time, Sarah," he said. "They'll heal more."

"The scars won't disappear," she said.

"I doubt that they will," he said, "but they'll get better."

The ritual of bandage changing had been replaced by ball squeezing early every morning, and Sarah dreaded it almost as much. Every day her mother demanded the number of squeezes be increased by one from the day before. By the time they got to ten in each hand, Sarah noted that she didn't feel much pain while she was doing it, although her hands ached for hours after each session. Her mother replaced the ball with a smooth wooden dowel. Squeezing it meant squeezing tighter than the ball of yarn demanded, fingers touching the scars on her palms. She had to admit it was helping, however. Sarah found herself able to do more with her hands then, even dressing herself, although she still needed help with buttons.

Winter passed into spring and spring into summer. With some of the profits from last year's flax harvest, Delina had hired a second man to help Hiram tend this year's crop. They tilled a larger field, and things looked promising for another good harvest. The gardens were also doing well. Sometimes Delina looked downright cheerful when she came back to Grandfather's after the Saturday visit.

17

Stroke

One Sunday Grandfather's stable man, Jeff, drove Delina and her children over to the farm. It was Sarah's first time there since the fire. Rags came rushing out to greet them. Rachel and Robbie hugged and petted the dog as he rolled over on his back for a belly-scratching.

The barn was completely obliterated. After one look, Sarah avoided glancing in that direction.

Robbie and Rachel spent the day rushing about, checking on their old haunts. Their mother went to inspect the flax crop, but everything Sarah saw reminded her of her father, and she was overwhelmed with sadness. She sat in the rocking chair on the porch. Everything was different — nothing would ever be the way it used to be.

It was early afternoon when Jeff came driving the buggy up the road, clouds of dust blowing up around him.

"Get in! Get in!" he yelled. "It's your grandfather!"

Delina rushed over, dragging Rachel and Robbie by the hands. Sarah jumped in. Jeff yelled to the horse, and they raced off.

"What happened?" Delina said, as they all held on for dear life.

"Stroke," he said.

"Dead?" she asked.

The groom shook his head. "He's not dead but —"

Sarah could say nothing. Her chest was tight with fear. She'd lost her father. She couldn't lose her grandfather, too.

"Doctor?" her mother asked as they raced around the corner to Broad Street.

"There now," Jeff said.

Sarah jumped off before Jeff had brought the horse to a complete standstill. Her mother was just behind her, and the others followed. Grandfather's maid, Stella, stood at the open door.

"Where?" Delina demanded.

"In the library."

They dashed into the room. The doctor was closing up his bag. Grandfather was seated in the big chair, an angry look on his face. One eye drooped. His mouth was drawn down on one side. He looked pale and, as they came in, he struggled to speak, "A-a-a-a-ah."

Sarah ran to him and hugged him fiercely. Seeing that the doctor and her mother were about to leave the room, Sarah patted her grandfather's hand and stood up. "I'll be right back, Grandfather," she said.

"Aaa-aa!" he said. There was no doubt that he meant no.

Her mother turned to come back inside the room. She said, "I don't think he wants us talking about him unless he can hear us."

He nodded slowly.

"All right," said the doctor. "Here it is. Henry, you've been afflicted by apoplexy. I know it's terrible, but you can get better. Most likely you will. You are tough and you're luckier than many —"

Grandfather made a sound of protest.

"Yes, you are, Henry," the doctor went on firmly. "You are luckier than many because you did not die during the stroke and because the paralysis seems limited to your right arm and leg and part of your face. You still have your senses. Many people die upon being struck. Still others struggle with half-use of their bodies or are totally paralyzed."

"Will he really get better?" Sarah asked.

"It's likely. He's got a strong will. There should be some sign of improvement within the next forty-eight hours or so. If you improve even slightly in the next two days, Henry, I shall be much encouraged."

Grandfather grabbed the doctor's hand with his left and then motioned to his throat.

"Will he be able to talk again?" Sarah asked.

"Possibly," said the doctor. "Give it time, Henry." He turned to Delina. "For now, let him rest. If he wants to lie down, you can move him, but no more than you have to. Give him clear broth and as much water as he wants. No spirits. Someone should be with him all the time. Goodbye, Henry." He turned to the others. "Send for me if there's a change."

Although Sarah and her mother tried at first to keep Robbie and Rachel from disturbing Grandfather, the old man seemed comforted by their presence. He drifted in and out of sleep, lying back against his pillows in the big chair as they played on the floor near him. Waking suddenly, he would look around wildly and then relax as he saw his family.

Afraid of missing the sign of improvement that the doctor had spoken of, Sarah and her mother stayed close by. Delina sewed and Sarah, now able to hold a book without difficulty, read as the steeple clock on the mantle measured the hours. That night, Sarah and her mother took turns with Jeff, sitting by Grandfather's chair as he dozed fitfully.

They were eating breakfast the next morning. Grandfather had been bathed and dressed. Jeff was feeding him his breakfast. Rachel and Robbie bounced in as cheerful as ever. Grabbing up a biscuit, Rachel went right in to her grandfather. The others continued their breakfast and then went into the library.

Rachel was perched on Grandfather's knee, chattering about the children she liked at school. Sarah and her mother smiled and settled in for another day of watchful care. Each was lost in her own thoughts, and it took several minutes for Rachel's talk to register.

"No, Grandfather," she said. "Say RAY chel. Ray, Ray, Rachel."

"Rachel," said her mother. "Don't tease Grandfather. He can't say it, but I'm sure he wants to."

"Yes, he can," Rachel said calmly. "He's almost got it right. Say it again, Grandfather."

"TTTTTTAAAACHCHCHCHCell," he said. The sounds stretched out of his mouth slowly. When he finished, his smile dipped down on the right side, but it was a smile. He knew what it meant. Sarah and her mother were beside him in a minute. Delina patted his shoulder awkwardly, but Sarah's hug was so exuberant that it knocked him back in the chair.

"Oh, Grandfather," she said. "It's going to be all right."

18

An Old Letter

Grandfather's recuperation from the stroke proceeded slowly. The family squealed with delight at each improvement, but he showed his frustration and impatience with the body that had betrayed him. There was some movement now in his right hand. He could walk a bit, leaning heavily on the cane and dragging his right foot, his right hand dangling. He could say words and phrases, although only a few came out clearly. His "NO!" was unmistakable. Through gestures and sounds, he made some of his wants known.

Rachel was the only one who understood most of what he said. The others got some words, but usually turned to Rachel for translation. The little girl beamed with pride at each success. It was also Rachel who could be heard often slowing up her own speech, over-pronouncing the words and encouraging her grandfather's attempts to echo them.

After the first week, Delina resumed her work at the factory, ignoring her father's protests. She left each morning wearing her usual plain work dress and apron, but to save time Jeff drove her to and from the factory in the carriage. She said that other mill girls looked on with amusement at the fine style in which she came and went. Delina paid them no mind but entered the factory with her head up and shoulders back as usual.

Delina insisted that living with Grandfather was temporary and that the money she made at the factory and only that money would be used to keep the farm going.

She resumed her visits back to the farm to supervise things and to tend to the accounts after work on Saturdays. Sometimes the children went over with her, mostly to make sure that Rags and Dorcas were all right. They wanted the dog with them at Grandfather's, but Hiram felt that Rags was needed to guard the farm.

For Sarah, that time with Grandfather as he continued to improve was a golden time. She still grieved for her father but surprised herself some evenings when she realized that days had passed without thought of him. Her worries about her grandfather were eased by the steady progress he was making.

Although she still felt self-conscious about her hands and hid them in front of strangers, they now worked quite well and, she had to admit, some of the redness had faded. Her eyebrows and eyelashes had filled in. The scar near her ear was hardly noticeable. She no longer avoided looking in a mirror.

Grandfather had hired a tutor for the children so

that the school problem was solved, and except for
lesson time they were free to occupy themselves. The
large lawns made wonderful playgrounds, and the
walks that wound through them made splendid
places for hopscotch games and hoop-rolling.

One day Sarah realized with a start that this must
be the life her mother had once led. She tried to imagine her mother as a child, surrounded by such beautiful things. She'd have thought that any child growing up surrounded by such beauty would be happy
and smiling all the rest of her life, but she couldn't
picture her mother running through the garden or
rolling hoops.

She went into the library. Grandfather was reading
in his chair. Sarah found it comforting to talk with
Grandfather, even though the conversation mainly
went one way if Rachel wasn't there to interpret.

"Grandfather," she said, "was my mother always
like this?"

His left eyebrow went up as he looked up from his
book, but he said nothing.

"I mean, when she was little, did she have fun?"

He nodded, smiling his lopsided smile.

"Ball," he said. "Jump rope." The words came out
slowly but clearly.

She hugged him. "Oh, Grandfather," she said.
"You sound just like your old self."

His look told her he didn't believe her for a minute, but he smiled again and stroked her hair with his good hand.

That night over supper, Sarah found herself staring at her mother, trying to picture her as a little girl with a jump rope in her hand.

"What is it, Sarah?" Her mother looked up and caught her stare.

"Nothing," she said. She drew her eyes back to her plate but couldn't resist looking at her mother out of the corner of her eyes.

Rachel took her role as translator for Grandfather quite seriously, even suggesting that she should be allowed to skip lessons because of it. Her mother's protest was as loud as her grandfather's to that proposal. Rachel had to be content with the few hours left each day. Sarah suspected that her sister made up some of the commands she insisted her grandfather had issued. Many times when the cook asked him what he wanted for supper, it turned out to be all of Rachel's favorites. Grandfather's eyes would sparkle and his lips would form his crooked smile on hearing some of Rachel's translations.

One cold Saturday in December, Rachel and Sarah had elected to stay at Grandfather's while Robbie went to the farm to meet his mother. Sarah, with Rachel's assistance, was going through the mail.

Although he could read, it was awkward for Grandfather to handle the envelopes and their contents. He preferred to have Sarah read the letters and notices aloud to him. Sometimes, halfway through, he would motion to read no further and throw it away. Other times the instruction, sometimes relayed through Rachel, was to file it in the large oak file cabinet in the office or even to compose a reply.

It was while Sarah was filing some correspondence that she saw an unopened letter to her grandfather under a small pile of papers on the top of the cabinet. Curious, she read a return address.

Jonathan Edmonds, Esq.
23 Beacon Street
Boston, Massachusetts
She knew she should take the letter to Grandfather, but in all the correspondence that had gone through her hands these last months, this was the only one from Boston, a place she associated only with her father. Carefully, she opened the seal.

September 30, 1851
My Dear Mr. Wilcox,
As per your recent request, I have been able to interview several passengers from the voyage of the Industry, *the ship having docked in Boston on*

*June 3, 1850. These men appeared to be of good
character. None of them had heard about the fate of
the subject of your inquiry, nor indeed did they know
the name of same. Further query indicated that they
had not heard of any such occurrence aboard ship.
Although the men were in steerage, each thought he
would have heard of such a tragedy even if it
occurred among passengers in a higher class.*

*Thus far, I have been unable to locate the captain
or any of the crew.*

*As you also directed, I have acquired the trunk
from the establishment of Josiah Trumbull. It awaits
your disposal here.*

*Should you desire my pursuance of this or any
other matter, I remain at your pleasure.*

Your obedient servant,

Jonathan Edmonds

Sarah sat down, holding the letter for a moment,
then she read it again. She knew nothing about travel
aboard ship and had no idea how many passengers
would have been on her father's last voyage. It did
seem likely that a crime or accident in which a pas-
senger lost his life would be the subject of much conversation on the ship or in any other company. Had
there been a mistake?

She put the letter in her apron pocket to wait for

her mother's arrival. As soon as she could get her mother alone, Sarah showed her the letter.

Delina Corbin read the letter quickly and immediately took the letter to her father and read it aloud to him, ignoring his moan and his gesture that indicated that she should stop reading after the first sentence. When she finished she looked at him wordlessly. He stared straight back at her.

"Is that about Father?" Rachel asked.

Her grandfather nodded slowly. He kept his eyes on his daughter.

"What does it mean?" Rachel's eyes were wide.

Delina said, "Do you know, Father?"

There was no answer.

"Are there other letters from Jonathan Edmonds?"

"No," he said.

"Did you know this letter had come?"

He nodded.

"Why didn't you open it?"

Sarah and her mother turned to Rachel after they tried and failed to understand his reply.

"Grandfather says he didn't get a chance," Rachel said.

His eyes had still not left his daughter's face.

"Rachel," Delina said. "Cook has just made ginger snaps. Robbie's in there now. Go and have some with him."

Rachel started to leave and then sat back again. "You'll need me to talk for Grandfather," she said.

"I think that between us, Sarah and I will manage this once," Delina said. She waited until Rachel had stomped out of the room.

"Is this Jonathan Edmonds a reliable person, Father?"

He nodded.

"You've used him before on other matters?"

"Yes," he said.

"There's been nothing further on this matter?"

"No."

"Then someone must follow through on this, Father," she said.

Grandfather slowly nodded.

19

Questions

"Mother, you are going to Boston, aren't you?"

"I am."

"When?"

"As soon as I get things in order here."

"May I go too?"

"No."

"Why, Mother? Why can't I go with you?"

"*I* shall go to Boston, Sarah."

"But maybe you'll find out about Father."

"Perhaps."

"I need to know."

"You will know what you need to know."

"I've never ridden on a train."

"True."

"You really should let me go be —"

Delina wheeled around to face her daughter.

"Enough!" she said. "I shall go to Boston, Sarah. I shall go alone. You will stay here." She strode into her room and firmly shut the door behind her.

Grandfather had instructed (through Rachel) that Delina was to have a new outfit for her trip. He would allow no objections. Delina would be calling on his associate there, and she would be fitted out as the daughter of Henry Wilcox should be. A dressmaker was summoned. Since Delina refused to pick out a style for her dress and coat, Grandfather found them in a magazine called *Godey's Ladies' Book*. Soon people arrived bearing packages containing stays and material for the dress and for petticoats. The house became a flurry of activity for the few days before Delina's trip.

On a Wednesday morning, Delina Corbin took the eight o'clock train to Boston, wearing a silk dress of black on tan plaid that fell just above her ankles. The cinched-in waist and the many petticoats made the skirt stick out like a flower. The warm wool coat was long and hung to just three inches above the length of the dress. The matching hat and gloves were just perfect. Sarah thought that her mother looked like any fine lady traveling to Boston for pleasure. She did wish her mother would walk as other ladies did, in such a way as to seem to be gliding across the floor, but Delina walked briskly with her accustomed stride in this outfit as in any other.

All that day during lessons, Sarah had trouble keeping her mind on what she was doing. Instead of the assigned math calculations, she calculated the timing of her mother's trip. It should take about four hours to get to Boston on the train, which could go as fast as thirty miles per hour. There would be stops at Springfield, Worcester, and Framingham. She imagined riding beside her mother, seeing those cities and all their wonders. Then pulling into Boston at last, her mother would head straight for the offices of Jonathan Edmonds, she was sure. What would he tell her? What was in her father's trunk? Would she find the captain of the *Industry*? Perhaps the ship was in port again and her mother could talk to the crew.

At last lessons were over. Grabbing a handful of cookies, Robbie and Rachel ran outside to play. Sarah sat with her grandfather in the library, gazing out the front window. He appeared to be absorbed in his book, but she saw him consulting his watch.

Sarah wandered over to the stereoscope and picked it up, looking at one slide after another without really seeing them at all. Then she stopped to examine one closely. The side-by-side pictures showed a woman descending from a train. It could almost be her mother, although this woman was younger, Sarah thought. Both pictures seemed exactly alike. With a straight edge, she measured the distance of the woman from the edge of each picture. The difference was the barest fraction of an inch, but there was a difference. She placed the pictures in the stereoscope and looked through the lens. The woman seemed to pop out from the train and the rest of the background. She pretended it was her mother, stepping off the train into Westfield. In her mind she tried to see her mother from her grandfather's point of view — a few steps to the right of her own view.

Did her grandfather see a little girl playing jump rope when he looked at his daughter? Sarah tried to see her that way, but the image of her stern mother jumping rope made her laugh. Just then the front door opened and her mother stepped into the room. Sarah was confused. Which image was real?

"Mother!" she cried, running to her. "What did you find out? Did you get the trunk? Did you find the captain?"

Delina opened her mouth to speak, but Robbie and Rachel came dashing in.

"Was it fun riding the train?" Robbie asked. "How fast did it go?"

"Was it scary in the big city? How many people did you see?" Rachel wanted to know.

Their mother drew a deep breath and took off her coat and hat. She hung the coat on the hall tree and laid her hat on the table beside it. She began removing her gloves. "Let me wash up," she said. "I'm covered all over with cinders and dirt from the train."

"But Mother —"

"I'll tell you all about it when I come down."

They stared after her as she went up the stairs to her room.

There was nothing for it but to wait. Fortunately

Delina didn't make them wait long. In a few minutes, she came back wearing her work dress, transformed into her usual self. Sarah knew the news would not be good. Her mother would have told them any good news right away. They followed Delina into the library. Grandfather leaned forward in his chair as she began her account.

"Mr. Edmonds knows no more than he told you in the letter, Father. He seems to have explored every avenue that might have revealed any information about Miles. No one Mr. Edmonds talked to knew anything about it. I have asked him to continue his search. For now, the best he could do is give me his trunk."

"Where is it?" Sarah asked. "Did you bring it?"

"I brought it. Jeff will bring it in," her mother said. She drew a deep breath. "There's a letter in it that — well, wait. We'll read it together."

"Did you talk to the captain of the ship, Mother?"

"No, Sarah. I went to the pier, but the ship was not in port."

"How — many — months?" Grandfather asked.

"How many months has the ship been gone, Father?"

He nodded.

"No one on the docks had seen it for a very long time. That's all they would tell me."

The library door opened, and Jeff entered bearing a trunk about two feet long and a foot or so deep. Two leather straps went from back hinges over the lid to the front and attached to buckles on the base. A broken lock dangled from the clasp. Jeff placed the trunk on the floor in front of Grandfather and left the room.

Her eyes filled with tears as Sarah ran her hand over the surface of the trunk. She could picture her father's large hands opening the trunk, placing inside his treasures, maybe even his gold. She knew that, whatever was inside, she would cherish the trunk itself forever.

Delina knelt and removed the padlock. They all leaned forward as she raised the lid and began taking out the contents — a chisel, a small hammer, a flat sort of copper dish, a shirt, a pair of pants, some blank paper, a pen and a bottle of ink and, lastly, an envelope.

"Is that all there is?" Sarah said. She'd laid such hope in the trunk. Surely it should have had something more important than this. Her mother held up the envelope. As she did so, Sarah noticed the address: Delina Corbin, Westfield, Massachusetts. It was her father's writing. She reached forward to touch it. After a brief pause, Delina opened the letter and began to read.

My Dear Delina and Children,
I have very good news. I have found gold. I've
booked passage on the Industry *to set sail 'round the*
Horn.
   I'll write again when we reach port.
Your loving husband and father,
Miles Corbin

"Date?" Grandfather asked.

"It is not dated, Father."

He raised his eyebrow.

"The other letters were dated, weren't they?"
Sarah asked, but she knew the answer. She'd read
those letters so often she could see them with her eyes
closed. Of course they were dated. She'd even looked
back in the scrapbook to see what they were all doing
on the days her father had written the other letters.

"Maybe he just forgot," she said.

"Perhaps," said her mother, "but it is strange.
Also, the letter's very brief. It doesn't sound like
Miles."

"And why didn't he mail it before he set sail?"
asked Sarah.

Her grandfather's head went up.

"Not right," he said.

"You're right, Father. It isn't right at all," Delina
said.

20

Surprise

Grandfather's recovery gathered speed as the next weeks went by. His speech was now nearly normal, an accomplishment Rachel took with a mixture of pride and remorse — pride because she knew she had played a part in the recovery and remorse because her vital role as interpreter was at an end.

For Sarah there was only joy. Grandfather was like his usual self. He could walk quite well, using the cane only a bit more heavily than before his stroke. His right foot lagged behind almost imperceptibly. The use of his right hand had also improved, although writing was still difficult.

With the physical problems at least partially overcome, Grandfather went about his business, checking on his investments and calling on associates.

"Father," Delina said, coming into the library one evening in early March, "it's time for us to go back to the farm."

There was complete silence as her children absorbed the statement. The farm was their home, but living with Grandfather was so easy. It was fun being waited on and having no chores to do. Sarah had enjoyed just being able to play. Work on the farm was hard.

"Delina, there's no need —," her father began.

"There is need, Father," she said firmly. "You've recovered and we need to be home." A look at her children told them that protest was not permitted.

"Don't worry, Grandfather," Rachel said. "We can come see you every day."

"We'll move back to the farm next Saturday evening," Delina said.

She was as good as her word, and the move back was accomplished quickly. Although they all missed the luxury of the big house, it was good to be back home again. They picked up their chores with little complaint, and real life began again.

A few weeks later, when it became necessary for Grandfather to make a trip to Worcester, he asked Sarah to accompany him.

Delina consented and Sarah was delighted. They would take the train and stay overnight in a hotel, the Grand Hotel, in Worcester — for Sarah two brand-new experiences at once.

This time it was her mother who decreed new clothes for the journey, and she insisted that the cost be taken from her own salary and profits from the farm. She gave the dressmaker a bolt of fine linen she'd obtained by barter with the textile mill in Woronoco — tiny pink flowers against a light blue background.

The dressmaker protested that a really fashionable outfit ought to be made of silk, but Delina said linen would do. They were, after all, farm people, not lords and ladies. She did, however, contract for three petticoats in addition to the over-petticoat, chemise, and underdrawers. After again consulting *Godey's Ladies' Book,* the dressmaker put together a suitable outfit for a young girl.

That morning Sarah rose early and donned her undergarments, silk stockings, and new shoes. She put on the new dress with its fan front bodice and capped, close-fitting long sleeves. Her full skirt fell in cartridge pleats. She put on the matching bonnet, eased the gloves over her scarred hands, and walked out, feeling quite the lady, to where Grandfather and Jeff waited in the carriage. She took Jeff's hand to be helped up to her seat, straightened her skirt demurely, and smiled down at Robbie and Rachel, waving as they drove off.

The train ride to Worcester was as wonderful as Sarah had hoped. From her seat by the window, she gazed out as they traveled through the mountains and alongside the river. She watched the little towns of Palmer and Brimfield whisk by as she caught a glimpse of little more than a few storefronts and a church. Her mother must have enjoyed her journey through here.

Sarah turned to her grandfather. "When did my mother change?"

"Change?"

"Yes, you said she had fun when she was little. When did she change?"

He sighed. "I don't know. Things happen. We all change. Who knows why?"

He paused for thought and then went on. "Her mother died when she was much younger than you are, Sarah. It was sudden. One day Grace seemed fine and the next . . . I suppose that changed Delina, losing her mother like that. It changed both of us. The servants took care of her. I had the business to tend to."

"Was she sad?"

"I suppose. Yes, of course she was sad. But she was a good little thing. I'm afraid I didn't pay much attention to her. Time passed. Next thing I knew she was running the household. And she was good at it."

"I'll bet she was." Sarah smiled.

"Then she met your father and nothing would do but that she marry him. There were others. But it was Miles she wanted and she was gone. Fortunately, she didn't go very far." He smiled. "And then there was you, and Robbie, and Rachel, and I had a family again. This time I had sense enough to enjoy it."

Sarah sighed when they pulled into Worcester

station, not yet having had her fill of such wonders and such conversation.

The depot at Worcester was crowded with travelers. Sarah stared about. There were even many women traveling alone! Porters hustled about after them with carts loaded with baggage. Imagine!

There was a mob of people at the station entrance waiting for hansom cabs. Fortunately Grandfather had hired a carriage in advance. If Grandfather's health was better they could have walked the few short blocks to the hotel. As it was, they were glad of the ride.

They were shown side-by-side rooms on the second floor overlooking the Blackstone River. Sarah's room was luxurious, but she had little time to enjoy it. She had only rinsed her face using the ornate pitcher and basin when she heard Grandfather's knock at the door.

"Ready to go to work, my dear?" he asked.

"Ready and willing," she said, taking his arm as they carefully descended the beautiful staircase into the lobby.

"Mr. Wilcox!" a well-dressed gentleman called out.

"Haines," Grandfather acknowledged. He turned to Sarah. "This may take a while, Sarah," he said. "That's Mr. Haines from the textile mills in Clinton."

"I'll just look around, then," she said as the two gentlemen shook hands.

Sarah went out the big glass doors of the hotel and stood there, enjoying what she could see of the city as night fell. A line of hansom cabs waited near the hotel entrance, the drivers chatting together at the corner while the horses stood patiently. They looked sad, Sarah thought, just standing in the street like that. Sarah reentered the hotel and stopped at the entrance to the dining room.

"Yes, Miss?" said the headwaiter. "May I seat you?"

"No, thank you," she said. "I wondered if I might have some cubes of sugar."

He smiled. "The horses?"

She nodded.

"One moment, Miss," he said, hurrying off. Soon he was back with a handful of sugar cubes. "Ask the drivers' permission," he cautioned.

Sarah thanked him and went back out to the cab rank. There were now five in line.

As she approached the group of drivers, one of them turned and walked quickly to the last cab in line and climbed in. Sarah saw him sit back into the shadows of the cab, but she caught a glimpse of his face as he turned quickly from the light.

"Father?" she gasped. "Father!" She ran toward

the cab, but he was off up the street at a fast trot. She stopped in mid-stride and stared after him.

She spoke sharply to herself. That man was not her father, only someone who looked a little like him. It had happened to her before. Several times in the long months since his death, Sarah had thought she'd seen him on the streets of Westfield, only to find, of course, that it was not her father at all. She'd only seen this man's face for an instant. It was surely not her father. Still, she realized, it wasn't just this man's face that seemed familiar. There was the way he walked, the way he swung up into the driver's seat. Everything he did was so like Miles Corbin. It couldn't be, and yet —

She turned and headed back to the hotel, the sugar cubes clutched in her hand. Grandfather was still engaged in conversation. Sarah sat in a chair on the other side of the window, gazing out at the hansom cab line and arguing with herself.

It wasn't her father. It couldn't have been. Miles Corbin was dead. He'd died off the Horn of South America. If he were alive, he'd be in Westfield right now, entertaining everyone with the stories of his adventures in California.

It was a good thing that Grandfather had not seen her running down the street yelling like that, making a fool of herself in such an unladylike way. He'd have been ashamed of her. She turned the sugar cubes over and over in her hand as she thought about it. She noticed that her glove was quite sticky. She put the cubes down on the table and brushed her gloved hand against her skirt, but it did no good. Sighing, she eased her gloves off her hands. She'd just have to hope no one noticed the scars.

Sarah did hope the driver hadn't seen or heard her yelling at him like that. Why, he'd think she was a crazy person instead of a fine lady accompanying her grandfather on such an important business trip. She looked out the window as a group of four ladies came out of the hotel and stood at the sidewalk. One raised her hand and the first cab driver in line pulled up to the door and helped two of them into the carriage. The next cab took the remaining two ladies. As those cabs pulled away, the others in line moved up to await the next customers. The man she had mistaken for her father had been at the end of the line. Why had he left so abruptly?

Sarah thought again about that embarrassing scene in the street. She pictured it in her mind. She had walked toward the men to get permission to feed the horses. One man had hurried to his carriage as she approached the group. That movement had caught her attention and she had watched him getting into the carriage. As he sat back into the carriage, the light from the hotel had caught his face for an instant. She saw that face again in her mind's eye. It was her father. It didn't make sense, but it was Miles Corbin.

No longer in doubt and unable to sit still any longer, she got up and went over to Grandfather.

"Grandfather?"

"Yes, my dear," he said. "I'm sorry to have kept you waiting. Sarah, this is Mr. Haines. Mr. Haines, my granddaughter."

"Happy to meet you," Mr. Haines said, bowing slightly.

Grandfather and Mr. Haines shook hands again. Mr. Haines approached the front desk, and Grandfather took her arm as they walked toward the door.

"That was a fortunate encounter," he said. "Haines —"

"Grandfather," she interrupted. She stopped walking and turned to face him. She drew a deep breath. "I just saw my father."

His eyebrow shot up. "Miles?" he asked. "Where?"

"Outside," she said. "Driving a hansom cab."

"Are you sure, Sarah?"

"Not really," she said. "I didn't get close to him, but it really did look like him."

"Is he still outside?"

"No, he drove off."

"Did he see you?"

"I don't know."

They stepped outside the hotel and approached three drivers who stood together at the curb.

"A ride, sir?" one asked.

"A moment first," Grandfather said. "Do any of you know Miles Corbin?"

The men shook their heads as they glanced at each other.

"Does he live around here, sir?"

"I don't know," Grandfather said. "My granddaughter thought she recognized him earlier driving a cab."

"Here?" asked one man.

Sarah nodded.

"Well, let's see," he said. "Who's been here tonight, boys? There was Charlie —"

"And Pete," said another. "Stan was here earlier, too."

"His horse was white," Sarah remembered suddenly. "It was the only white horse here."

"Oh, that's Mike," said one of the men. "He's a good sort, Mike is."

"Thought his name was Matt," said another.

"No, I think it's Mike."

"What's his last name?" Grandfather asked.

"Dunno, sir," said the first man. "No need, you know?"

"Have you known him long?" asked Grandfather.

The man shrugged. "He started up a few months ago."

"Where does he live?" Sarah asked.

"Don't know, Miss."

Sarah took a short, quick breath. "Is he coming back?" Sarah asked.

The man shrugged. "Can't tell, Miss," he said. "Depends on the fares and where they want to go. It's a busy day. Lots of folks in town this week."

"Yes, yes," Grandfather said impatiently. "I'd like to engage you for the evening," Grandfather said, pointing to the man whose carriage was first in line.

"Very good, sir," he said, helping them in as the others turned back to their conversation.

"Where to?" he asked, seating himself and picking up the reins.

"Find Mike," Grandfather said.

"But I don't know —"

"Go wherever you think he might be."

"That could run up a pretty big fare," the man said doubtfully.

Grandfather took out his money clip and extracted ten dollars. He handed it to the driver. "This should do for a while," he said.

"Right you are, sir," the driver replied, and they started down the street.

At each intersection, Sarah leaned out to look as far as she could down the street on her side while Grandfather did the same on his own. They saw several other cabs, but none was drawn by a white horse. They traced and retraced routes around the city.

It was quite late and most of the streets were clear when the driver turned. "We've been most everywhere, sir," he said. "We can go on, but you'll be wasting your money. All the cabs but us have put up for the night."

Grandfather thought a moment. "Take us back to the hotel. I'm sorry, my dear," he said, turning to Sarah, "but tomorrow's another day."

"Just a bit longer?" Sarah couldn't bear to think of a whole night's passing without knowing for sure.

He shook his head. "I'm tired, Sarah. My strength isn't what it once was. We'll try again tomorrow. This Mike, if that's his name, will be out on the street again and we can hunt in the daylight."

Of course he was tired and so was Sarah, now that she thought about it. It had been a very long day. She nodded and they returned to the hotel.

After bidding her grandfather good night, Sarah

carefully removed her clothes and hung them in the wardrobe. She washed, and put on her nightclothes. Then she lay on the bed, sure that she'd be unable to sleep.

When she heard a knock at the door, she was surprised to see that it was morning. Heavens! And here she was still in her nightdress.

"Oh, Grandfather," she said, unlocking her door and opening it, "I'm —"

Her father stood in the doorway.

21

Some Answers and a Question

For a moment, Sarah just stood, staring at him. As if to assure herself that she wasn't dreaming, she reached out to touch her father's sleeve. As she did, her father stepped forward and hugged her.

"Oh, Sarie," he murmured. "My dear sweet Sarie."

Oh, the comfort of those arms. She clung to him, her cheek rubbing against his rough coat. She cried and then sobbed with joy and relief. When she lifted her head she could see that his face was as wet as her own.

He smiled down at her. "I wasn't sure you'd be that glad to see me."

"Not glad!" she said. "You're alive. Why wouldn't I be glad?" Then she pulled back as cold reality took over. "Why? Father, why?"

"Why am I alive?" He grinned.

"No jokes!" She pounded at his chest as her joy turned to anger. "Why?"

At that moment the door to the adjacent room opened. Grandfather stepped into the hall and then turned to see them.

"Miles?" he said. "Good God!" He stepped back

a moment and then came forward angrily. "Explain yourself."

Her father nodded. "I was about to try to do just that," he said. "Can we go inside and sit down? This may take a while."

Grandfather unlocked his door. "In here," he said.

They took chairs around a small round table at the window. Sarah leaned forward to stare at her father across the table. She put out a hand to touch him again and then drew back as she realized he'd see the scars.

Grandfather's face was stern. "Well?" he demanded. "This better be good," he added.

Miles Corbin shook his head. "It isn't," he said. "It isn't very good at all."

He looked directly at Sarah.

"You saw me last night, didn't you, Father? That *was* you in the cab line, wasn't it? Why did you run away?"

"At first I couldn't believe it was you coming toward me," he said. "You looked so beautiful — all grown up, Sarah. When I realized that it was you, I ran. I was going to disappear — go to some other town, but I couldn't do it. It's no good hiding anymore. I knew I had to find you and try to explain."

He looked at them both and, finding no comfort in either face, he drew a deep breath and began his tale.

"Getting to California took a long time," he said. "Did you get the letters I sent?"

Sarah nodded.

"Well, I'd spent all my money just getting there. Then I had to buy the equipment," he said. "Everything was so expensive. Before I even got to the river to start panning for gold, I'd built up quite a debt."

"A debt," Grandfather said. "What a surprise."

Miles smiled ruefully. "I know," he said. "But those suppliers —"

"All right," Grandfather said. "You borrowed money for supplies and went to the middle fork of the American River."

Miles looked up, puzzled. "How did you —" He answered his own question. "My letter."

"Yes," said Grandfather. "One of those precious few letters your family got before the one announcing your death. Get to it, Miles."

As she sat there, Sarah's face became as stern as her grandfather's. He was alive. He'd been alive through their fire, Grandfather's stroke — all that pain. He could have helped. How could he have made them suffer so?

"Did you find any gold at all?" she asked.

"I did," he said. "I found quite a bit, actually. It's not easy, you know. You have to —"

"We can read a book about how to find gold," said Grandfather. "What we need from you is exactly why you deserted your family."

Her father nodded. "You're right. You're right of course," he said. "It's just that it's so hard . . ."

That was too much for Grandfather. "Hard?" he shouted, getting to his feet. "You had it hard, did you? What about your family, sir! Sarah nearly died! Robbie too! They had it hard! Your children needed you. My daughter needed you! Where were you?" His face was red and his hands shook.

"Please sit down, Grandfather," said Sarah. "Your health —" She put her hands on her grandfather's arm.

"Sarah," her father said. "Your hands —" He reached for them. "What happened?"

She shook her head, drawing them back. "Not now," she said. "Sit down, Grandfather."

Grandfather reseated himself, breathing deeply. Sarah fetched him a glass of water from the pitcher on the side table.

Her father waited and then spoke softly, "I mean it's hard telling you about it. I know I've made my family suffer. I know none of you can ever forgive me. I'm just trying to explain what happened."

"Then get on with it," Grandfather said.

Miles drew a deep breath. "I panned for gold for a

month, taking time only to sleep a few hours and then starting in again," he said. "At first I found quite a bit, but after the first week there were only a few flakes each day. There were so many prospecting for gold on that river that there just wasn't enough to keep going. I took what gold I had into the assayer's office to see how much it was worth." He looked down at his hands. "There wasn't enough."

"Enough for what?" Grandfather asked. "Enough to pay your creditors?"

"Well," her father said, "there was enough to pay the creditors there and to book passage on a ship home, but nothing more."

"You paid them, then."

"I paid all the creditors in California."

"Then why didn't you come home?" Sarah asked. "Why didn't you come back to us?"

"I was so ashamed," he said, looking up. "I'd taken all the family's money and borrowed more. I had been so sure I'd come home with gold enough to support us in style for years. But I had nothing left. Not even enough to pay back the friends and neighbors who'd staked me. Not a blessed thing but sore hands and a bent back." His head went down again.

"And when did you hit on the brilliant idea of defrauding your family?" Grandfather asked, his voice as cold as his face.

"On board ship," her father said. "I didn't mean to defraud. I only thought they'd be better off without me." He turned to Sarah. "For a while I thought of really jumping overboard. I'd tried so many times and failed so many times and disappointed your mother so often, Sarah. I thought that if I was dead, you'd go on with your lives."

"Living on what?" Grandfather said. "Your broken-down farm? Living on what?"

"You helped them, didn't you?" Miles asked. "I was sure you would."

"Very little," the old man said. "Delina's a proud woman. She'd take only a little from me."

"She's working in the whip factory," Sarah said, her eyes on her father's face.

"The whip factory! Delina?"

"My daughter is a mill hand, thanks to you, Miles Corbin," Grandfather said. "See what you've brought her to? You and your wild goose chases!"

"Did she lose the farm?" her father asked softly.

"No," Sarah said. "But the barn caught fire and Robbie was in it and he nearly died."

"Sarah went into the fire and brought him out," said Grandfather.

"My brave Sarah," said her father.

"And Mother's paid off all the debt. The farm's really doing quite well. We had a good flax crop."

"Flax?" asked her father.

"We can talk about the farm later." Grandfather interrupted. "Let's get back to your actions, Miles. You were on board ship and —"

"And two of the passengers got to fighting over a poker game. One threatened to take all the gold and throw the other overboard. He didn't, of course, but I thought, What if he had thrown me overboard? Wouldn't my family be better off without me? I just didn't have the courage to do it myself."

"That wouldn't have been courage," her grandfather said.

Her father sighed. "Well, whatever it would have been, I didn't do it. I got a friend to write the letter posing as the captain, telling you I'd been thrown overboard." He turned to Sarah. "I meant to disappear forever. I knew it was awful. I hated to upset you . . ."

"Upset! You thought they'd be upset, did you?" Grandfather was getting himself riled up again.

Sarah patted his hand, and he sat back. "Go ahead," he said to Miles. "Finish it."

"I wrote another letter and left it in my trunk," Miles said. "I wanted you to think I'd been successful." He looked pleadingly at Sarah. When she said nothing, he continued. "When the ship landed, I just walked away. I should have stayed in Boston, but there were just too many people — all that noise and commotion. Besides," he said, turning to Grandfather, "I knew you had many connections in Boston and I didn't want to take the chance of running into you or someone who knew you. I started walking west following the railroad tracks, doing odd jobs for my keep from time to time. I didn't want to get to where people would know me, but I came here to Worcester and I got a job driving a cab. It paid all right, and it meant being with a horse again and that was good. It's still a big city, though. I miss the farm."

"Oh," said Grandfather in a voice dripping with sarcasm. "How unfortunate, Miles. You're lonely, even unhappy, perhaps?" His voice changed to thunder. "Your family is in torment and you . . . you —" He could find no words to express his contempt.

Sarah looked at her father and then to her grandfather. Suddenly it was all too much. She had to think and think alone. She got up and left the room, but not before she heard her grandfather start in again. "Now let me tell you —" he said as she closed the door.

In the quiet of her own room, Sarah sat in the chair overlooking the river, trying to absorb it all. It was too much. Her father was alive. She should be feeling so glad. She'd missed him so. But he had deceived them all. She tried to match up the wonderful, kind, loving, gentle father she loved with the liar and deserter who sat in the next room. He'd been a coward — there was no other word for it — afraid to face them because he hadn't found gold, and they had needed him so much.

Adding cowardice to the picture of her father changed things. It was like the stereoscope: the second picture adding depth to the first. She could see her father for what he was — a coward and a liar — but there was the other image: the one she'd always had of him.

She thought about her mother. There wasn't much laughter in the image of her mother. But she had taken charge, hadn't she, after her husband left? She had kept them all together, making do. Delina Corbin, who was raised in such luxury, had done backbreaking work to keep her family together — had done it, Sarah realized with a start, even before her husband left. She had paid off her husband's debts and managed the farm into a profitable business.

Sarah wondered what her mother would do when she heard her husband was not dead. She really didn't have to wonder. She knew the reaction: Delina Corbin would be furious. She'd sputter, and she'd face it as she did everything else — head-on.

Doing the same, Sarah knocked softly on her grandfather's door. "It's open!" her grandfather said.

Entering the room, she found the two men just as she had left them, glowering at each other.

"Father," she said, "will you come back with us?"

"Sarah . . ." her grandfather sputtered. "I don't know if —"

Sarah kept her eyes on her father. "Will you come back with us?" she repeated.

Her father seemed to draw back into the chair. He shook his head slowly. "Sarie love, maybe someday I'll go back, but I'm not ready yet. I don't think —"

"I think you must come, Father," she said. "And you must come now. Robbie and Rachel and Mother, they don't deserve to hear about this from me or from Grandfather. They deserve to hear your, your —" She searched for the word.

"Excuses," her father spoke before her grandfather could. "But there really are none, are there? None that are good enough. I didn't find enough gold. I've let everybody down. They'll want no part of Miles Corbin."

"The thing is," Sarah said, "they do want — or at least I do want a part of Miles Corbin — any part of you I can get."

He stood up. "You forgive me?" His voice was incredulous.

"I don't know," she said. "I don't know if I forgive you. I don't even know if that's possible. You're my father, and I know that I've missed you and that I want you to come home. Is that forgiving?" She turned to her grandfather. "Is it?" she asked. "How about you, Grandfather? Can you forgive him?"

"It doesn't matter whether I forgive him or not," the old man said. "Under other circumstances . . ." — he glanced over at his son-in-law before going on — "except for this cursed stroke, and watching Sarah and Robbie suffer from the fire, I've enjoyed every golden minute of the last year. It's up to your family, Miles, to take you in or cast you out. It's the same with me either way. I'll help as much as Delina will let me." He raised one eyebrow as he looked at her father. "Well, Miles," he said, "ready to face Delina?"

Miles sat with his lips pressed tightly together. Then he said, "Well, I have seen the elephant. Now let's see if I can face the tiger."